A Diversity of Death

A Cotton Cunningham Academic Mystery

Dennis Collins

NFB Publishing
Buffalo, New York

Copyright © 2024 Dennis Collins

Printed in the United States of America

A Diversity of Death: A Cotton Cunningham Academic Mystery
Collins- 1st Edition

ISBN: 978-1-953610-79-9

1. Fiction>Hard-Boiled Fiction
2. Fiction>Crime
3. Fiction>Thriller>Suspense
4. Fiction>Murder Mystery
5. Fiction>Mystery
6. Fiction>Mystery Series

This is a work of fiction. All characters in this novel are fictitious. Any resemblance to actual events or locations, unless specified, or persons, living or dead is entirely coincidental.

No part of this book may be reproduced or transmitted in any form by any means, electronic or mechanical, including photocopying, recording, or by any information storage and retrieval system without permission in writing by the author.

NFB
<<<>>>
No Frills Buffalo/Amelia Press
119 Dorchester Road
Buffalo, New York 14213

For more information visit
NFBPubishing.com

This book is dedicated to
Leah, Heather, Evan, Caroline, Ruth,
Rory, Esme and Cindy

Cotton Cunningham Academic Mystery Series
by Dennis Collins

A SEMESTER OF DEATH

It was 1967, the year of the summer of love in San Francisco, but in Buffalo, New York, it was a year of rioting, looting, racial tension and later on, at the University of Buffalo, a little bit of murder. It was a year that saw visits by Jackie Robinson, Martin Luther King, and Mohammed Ali. Great rifts developed between faculty, students, administrators, and former Buffalo police detective and newly hired History professor, Cotton Cunningham was caught right in the middle of it.

DEATH CALLS THE DEAN

Mystery continues on the University of Buffalo campus as the death of a dean in 1968 is connected to the murder of a student twenty years before. Inter-office intrigue is at the forefront as Cotton Cunningham follows clues that will lead him from post-World War II times to the protest-filled years of the late sixties.

A Diversity of Death

Chapter 1

The University of Buffalo
January 20th

Jesse Parker rolled down Main Street in Buffalo with a satisfied grin on his face. He and his wife had sacrificed a lot to get where they were in life. His bachelor's degree from NYU, a PhD program in Mathematics at Northeastern in Boston, adjunct positions in the math departments in multiple colleges and finally a first-year position at the University of Buffalo. It would have been hard for anyone to achieve, but for Jesse, who was Black, it was monumental. His wife, Connie, had sacrificed also. Delaying the start of a family, their countless moves to different cities were difficult, but made easier by her chosen vocation. Connie was a pediatric nurse, and it was easier for her to gain employment. Her stints at Mount Sinai in New York and at Mass General in Boston gave her the credentials to pick her Buffalo hospital job. She chose Buffalo General Hospital.

Jesse's employment journey was much more complicated. Many universities were paying lip service in the employment of minorities. Blacks were present at most colleges, but they were sweeping floors or serving in cafeterias. They were secretaries, delivery men, maintenance, but very few in tenure track teaching positions. The University of Buffalo seemed different. It was city school and not some suburban campus where a Black man stood out. UB had Black students, Black guidance counselors, Black athletes, and even Black student organizations. UB's president, Martin Meyerson, was forward thinking, having been in administration at Berkley in California during a period called the Free Speech Movement. His interview with Meyerson went splendidly. It seemed like UB was interested in being in on the cutting edge of faculty diversity. He met other faculty members in both the math department and other sciences. People seemed congenial, but somewhat old fashion. Jessie wondered how he would fit in.

When he received news of his appointment, first in a letter and the in a meeting with the chair of the math department, he felt a mixture of elation and trepidation. He and Connie went out to celebrate at John's Flaming Hearth on Military Road in the town of Niagara. The Hearth was upscale and was famous when Soviet Premier Alexei Kosygin and a group of Soviet and American officials dined there in 1969. It was too expensive, but they needed to celebrate.

It was now two weeks into the spring semester and Jesse was beginning to get into a routine – leave the house about an hour before his ten o'clock class, stop of at *Your Host* for a coffee to go and perhaps a pastry. This morning it was more crowded than usual and, on the way out he was jostled and what... – a small twinge in his back? What was that? A leftover from a hard basketball game at the YMCA two nights ago? He was out the door and into his car on his way to the Main Street campus of the University of Buffalo.

Main Street shops passed by – gas stations, Mom and Pop grocery stores, pawn shops, the architectural detritus of urban renewal. He never really noticed them – they were a peripheral background to his daily campus drive. But now, they seemed different. Now they were moving, shifting, out of focus. The road ahead of him heaved up and dropped suddenly. His hands trembled on the wheel. Other automobiles swerved to avoid colliding with his 1959 Dodge Rambler. He could hear horns blaring in his ears and distant shouting. The last thing he could remember was water shooting into the air from a fire hydrant before he smashed into a car dealership window.

Chapter 2

February 2

Cotton Cunningham and Jefferson Drew were sitting in Drew's basement office with a bag from Freddie's Donuts between them. The weather was relentless-snow, snow and more snow. It was typical for this time of the year in Buffalo. The wind was a constant background noise and a companion to the clatter of the basement pipes. Cunningham was dressed in khakis and a heavy overcoat. Drew was in security clothes with neatly pressed slacks and gloves with the tips cut off.

They were discussing the various aspects of student unrest on campus and if that wasn't enough, some unusual problems that were cropping up at UB.

"When Jesse Parker ran off the road, I thought it was an isolated incident," said Cotton.

"Then," said Drew, "other occurrences popped up - Lavelle Hughes in sciences, Greg Barton on my security force and just last week Winston Scales on President Regan's staff. Only Parker died, but the rest could have been fatal."

The turn of the year at UB was a cataclysmic shift for both Cotton and Jefferson Drew. President Martin Myerson, whom the two had worked with very closely in clearing up many a problem in the last few years, was to be hired as the new president at the University of Pennsylvania. Although Meyerson had enjoyed his tenure at UB, the move was an obvious one because of his deep ties to the Philadelphia area. He was now on a leave of absence and Dr Peter Regan was taking his place. Meyerson, Cunningham, and Drew had a seamless relationship which had aided them in solving two crimes on the campus in previous semesters, one involving an assassination attempt on Muhamed Ali and the other a conspiracy by several professors to cover up the murder of a student. Their relationship with Regan was not as smooth.

Lavelle Hughes taught introductory chemistry courses. Somehow chemicals were switched around in his lab. At the last second, he realized the switch. If he would have continued, an explosive compound could have been produced. Hughes taught general chemistry

Greg Barton just missed being hit by a speeding automobile while stepping off a curb on Main Street across from the college. The vehicle had continued without stopping. It could have been a careless student or something more ominous.

Winston Scales was mugged in an Allentown alley and if it weren't for a bystander interfering, could have been seriously hurt.

"Were these isolated incidents or were they somehow connected?" asked Drew while fumbling with papers connected to the three occurrences.

"Connected by color," said Cunningham. "What are the chances of that?"

"What does Regan say," asked Drew, munching on a Boston Cream doughnut.

"I've only spoken to Regan once since Meyerson took

his leave of absence and the talk was amicable. He said he knew that Meyerson and the two of us were close and that we worked together. He knew that I was Meyerson's representative to the student body. He said that he would like to keep me in that capacity, but he wanted to keep my involvement in criminal affairs kept to a minimum. Something about me being a college professor and how I should stick to that."

"And the isolated incidents….?

"He thought that they were just that and that the college had enough problems without inventing them."

"He's right about that," said Drew. "I think that these past semesters were just a fuse leading up to this year. Look at all our problems -Project Themis, The Buffalo 9, ROTC, issues with the Blacks on the basketball team and the war in Vietnam. There is a demonstration on any one of the above on any given day. I left my job on a city police force so I could get away from all this. This job is way beyond that."

"To make matters worse, I get the feeling that Regan will not hesitate to call in the Erie County Sheriff's Department if he thinks things are boiling over. I know Meyerson was hesitant to do that. Regan's scheduled another meeting with me for tomorrow. I'll know more about where we stand then." said Cotton.

"Keep me in the loop," said Drew.

"I will," said Cotton. "And I agree with you. If we can get out of this semester in one piece, we'll be lucky."

Chapter 3

February 3
President's Office

"Come in, Cunningham, Would you like coffee? My secretary can handle that."

"No, I'm fine, Dr. Regan." Cotton was already caffeinated out even though it wasn't lunchtime.

He was struck by how much a person's office decor could reveal about his personality. Meyerson's office was warm, full of antique furniture that was stately and comfortable. There were paintings of river scenes and other objects of art. Pictures of family and friends abounded. Bookshelves were full on both sides of the room.

Regan's furniture was modern with more chrome and glass. The desk was institutional with pictures of family. Regan's background was in the medical field with an emphasis on psychiatry. As such, his library tended to be more towards the sciences. His hair was short in keeping with his previous experiences in the Army during both World War II and the Korean conflict. He wore glasses and was dressed in slacks, a white shirt and thin blue tie. His sport jacket was hung on a rack in the corner of the room. His manner was friendly but cautious.

"I know that you and Martin had a close relationship and he trusted you as his ambassador to the student body.

I'll be frank. I think he gave you way too much leeway to conduct your affairs. I'm looking for a relationship that will be much simpler. You will still be a conduit to the student body, but not in a criminal investigative capacity. I'm aware of your background with the Buffalo police and how that was helpful in solving some past problems, but I think that in the future those problems will be better handled by security and if necessary, by city authorities."

Cotton was silent for a moment. In a way, he was quite satisfied to be strictly a college professor, teaching courses, serving on committees, and doing research. He hadn't gone out of his way to pursue the unfortunate events that had sprung up in the previous two years. Meyerson's original intent was to have Cotton handle the mundane problems that sprung up between students and administration. Somehow, things had gone sideways, and Meyerson had come to rely on Cotton's background in the Buffalo police force to solve some serious problems. Cotton would much prefer to teach.

"Don't get me wrong," said Regan. "I want you to work with the student body. You can be very useful in that capacity, especially with the problems erupting in the past few months. The destruction wreaked upon the ROTC offices last October could have been prevented if a dialogue would have been established beforehand. I am always willing to meet with factions of the protest movement, but this administration will not tolerate roving barbarism. I will not have a significant portion of the student population living in fear. I believe it is a very small segment of our young people who are willing to resort to violence. I want you to be a conduit to that small segment and head off any violence before it spreads."

"I understand sir and I will do my best" Cotton said.

"Good. This semester will be critical. I know I'm not the only one to feel that something is brewing not only here but at campuses across the country. Let's try to keep UB out of the headlines," Regan said.

Cotton left the building feeling perplexed. He was happy to deal with students, but his mind was on the incidents with the minority faculty members. He knew it was useless to bring the matter up because Regan made it clear that such affairs were the province of the police, but there was one thing that Cotton was sure of. He did not want the Erie County Sherriff's Department on campus. That was just what his old friend Mike Amico wanted.

Cotton had worked with Amico when he was a detective with the Buffalo Police Department. Amico was now Erie County Sheriff with quite a few deputies under his command. He had little respect for how the Buffalo Police or the UB security force were handling the problems on campus. Amico believed that activists on the UB campus were responsible for major drug dealings in the Buffalo area. He thought that if he could get onto campus he could uncover and deal with this problem. Cotton thought this preposterous. He knew that drugs were common on campus, but to suggest that UB students were responsible for major drug dealings was way off base.

Still, Cotton thought that the latest incidents of violence towards minority candidates was something that he wanted to investigate further. The cop in him was creeping up.

As he walked back to his office at Diffendorf Hall, the winter wind buffeted him. Nothing was as unpredictable as Buffalo weather. Situated on Lake Erie, Buffalo was prone to serious lake effect snowstorms at a moment's notice. If the lake wasn't frozen over and it wasn't at this moment, the results could be disastrous. There were always students who wouldn't give up their summer shorts, traveling the short distance between dorm and classroom, but most of the students dressed wisely in faded bell bottom jeans, sweaters, and boots.

He was wearing a Navy pea coat, with muffler and watch cap. He was ready for the winter, but not quite ready for what the winter would bring.

Chapter 4

February 6
The Swannie House

Cotton was having drinks with Jen Valley at the Swannie House on Ohio Street, within walking distance of Memorial Auditorium and right in the middle of the warehouse district.

"How did things go with Regan?" asked Jen.

"He's not Meyerson, that's for sure," said Cotton sipping on a Pabst Blue Ribbon.

"In what way?" she asked.

"He's from the sciences. He looks at things in a certain cool, analytical way. Martin was always questioning. Willing to compromise, listen to the other side. Regan is, up to a point. The problem is he said he wouldn't hesitate to call out Mike Amico's men. Martin never thought that was part of the solution."

"Cotton, we need to talk….

"And Regan thinks that I should be more concerned at being his ambassador to the students than being a policeman….

"Cotton, there's something I want to…

"But I think that the recent attacks on minority faculty should be investigated…

"Cotton, shut up, will you!"

That certainly brought an end to his monologue.

"Cotton, I think I'm pregnant."

Cotton stared at her, speechless, his beer having slopped over the table.

"I haven't had my period for quite a while. I have a doctor's appointment tomorrow to make sure. If I am, it brings up a lot of issues."

Cotton finally found his tongue.

"I guess it does," said Cotton, still reeling with the news. "We need to get married."

"Hold on, hold on," said Jen. 'Just a while ago we were examining the pros and cons of moving in together. Now you're talking marriage. We've got a lot to discuss before the question of marriage come into the picture."

"Maybe I'm traditional," said Cotton. "I just believe that children should be raised in a setting where both parents are totally committed to one another. And the best setting is marriage."

"Cotton don't get me wrong. I think we're both committed to each other and that will eventually lead to marriage. I'm just not sure of the timing. I think living together before marriage is important. Getting used to each other. Now it's all going to be rushed. I just feel a mix of emotions. I'm happy, scared, anxious all in one."

"Ok, let's take this one step at a time," said Cotton. "First let's find out whether you are pregnant and then discuss living arrangements. I guess, we would either find a larger apartment or one of us moves in with the other. We can start getting serious about looking for houses, and we can even rent a house in the city. That might be the quickest way to deal with the situation."

"Cotton, you're so pragmatic, but that's not all I want to hear. It's something more than that."

Cotton looked perplexed.

"I want to know how you feel about us," she said.

Finally, he understood.

"Jen, know that I love you with all my heart and that I will follow you anywhere."

She smiled.

"That's all I wanted to hear."

Chapter 5

February 5
Bob Williams

Cotton was sitting in his office with his feet on his desk. He wasn't getting any work done because he couldn't concentrate. He was waiting for Jen to call with the results from the doctor's appointment. He hadn't slept much the night before, wondering about a myriad of things connected to his possible parenthood.

What kind of a dad would he be? Better than his dad for sure. Cotton's dad had died the year before, and Cotton was still dealing with issues from that. His father was a failure in Cotton's eyes. A steel worker by trade, a drunk who was promiscuous and highly critical of family members. He was in his glory when Cotton was a cop, but when his son decided to become an academic, he was on the verge of disinheriting him. To him, being a cop was macho and something he could brag about to "the guys."

When Cotton's sister gave birth to a Down Syndrome child, he was particularly cruel, announcing to the world that the "retard" would be nothing more than a burden to the family. In short, he was a come home, demand his supper, sit down in front of the TV with a beer, fall asleep in the recliner type of guy. What made matters worse was

Cotton had never come to terms with his father. On his father's death bed his only emotion was a huge wave of unfulfilled anger and disappointment.

He knew that he would not be anything like his father. The mold would be broken, and he would be involved. The son would cast off the father.

He was jarred out of his reverie by a knock on his door. A tall, spindly Black man, dressed in a UB team sports jacket with a t-shirt showing underneath, filled the door frame. He had on jeans with high top sneakers.

"Professor Cunningham, my name is Bob Williams. I don't have an appointment, but I wonder if I could speak with you for a moment?"

Cotton rose from behind his desk and extended his hand.

"Sure, have a seat," he said.

His visitor's voice had a strong Southern twang to it, and he moved gracefully across the room and settled in a chair, which did not come close to being comfortable.

"I'm coming to you because I've heard that you have a direct line to President Regan. I represent the Black basketball players and we believe that the coaches of the UB basketball team have been insensitive to our demands."

"I read the article in The Spectrum. I believe they called it "'gross insensitivity.'"

"Yea, well, call it what you would like, but Coach Serfustini is stonewalling us. We've had negotiations, but nothing has come of it."

Cotton tented his hands. "What are your demands?"

"They sprung a 1.60 academic requirement on us that we didn't see coming. If we're not on the team, then some of us would be in danger of losing our scholarship money.

We would also like to see the team moving towards hiring a black assistant coach – someone more in tune with our needs. We got a verbal agreement on that issue, but now they're backing off. We are now boycotting until our demands are met."

"I read that you're asking for the firing of Coach Serfustini , Moto and Baschnagal." said Cotton.

"That's true, "said Williams. "We believe that we have been mistreated to such an extent that we cannot go forward dealing with the same people. We've been lied to."

"Serfustini is a sports legend around here," Cotton remarked. "There is no way that he will be removed."

"He's leaning towards retirement," said Williams. "But they're just going to promote Motto and we're going to have the same problems. We're calling on other organizations to help us with our protests. EPIS Upward Bound, the Black Student Union and the Association of Black Athletes of Greater New York have all promised to back us. I'm looking for your support also."

Cotton leaned forward. "All I can promise is to relay your concerns to President Regan. I don't know the coaching staff on a personal level, so I have no frame of reference to form an opinion on your grievances. I do think they need to be heard and I'll do my best to relay that to Regan."

Williams rose out of his chair with a grim look on his face.

"Sounds like the same bullshit that I've heard from everyone at the college. We sympathize with you, but there's not much we can do. SDS and YAWF will demonstrate with us, but those white groups always want something out of the deal. "

He turned around and left without another word.

Chapter 6

Later that day

The call came in just after his afternoon class was over.

"Cotton, the test came up positive. You're going to be a father."

Cotton steadied himself against his desk. For some reason he had already decided that the test would turn up positive, but still, the realization had his head swimming.

"Cotton, are you there?" Jen asked.

"Yes, I'm here and I think it's great news and we should go out and celebrate."

"I think we should too. Where did you have in mind?"

"How about *Your Host*. I think I need some comfort food."

They met that evening in the middle of a raging snowstorm. Cotton picked up Jen even though the restaurant was just a few blocks from her Allentown walk up. By the time they found a parking space and walked the fifty yards to the restaurant, they were covered with snow.

"Maybe we should have stayed at my apartment and warmed up some soup, "said Jen.

"Nope," said Cotton. "We need to celebrate. "

They found a booth opposite a long counter full of patrons of all kinds – steel workers, with tools attached to their jeans, motorcycle club members with ponytails and keys on long chains attached to their belts, hospital workers in their scrubs, secretaries in professional dress and professorial college types wearing corduroy jackets with patches on their elbows. In the bright lights illuminating their faces, they were all dining on *Your Host* comfort food – mashed potatoes and meat loaf, spaghetti with meatballs, macaroni, and cheese and with the ever-present bottomless cup of coffee that *Your Host* always advertised. It was a twenty-four-hour haven for the everyman.

Cotton had the "WOW" sandwich. It was advertised as 28 and 1/2 square inches of top-quality sliced beef smothered with French fried onions and a specially baked roll, garnished with crisp pickle chips. Jen ordered an Old Fashion Breakfast with scrambled eggs and toast and a cup of tea.

"Not having a dinner?" asked Cotton.

"Upset stomach," she whispered.

"I'm sorry. Maybe we should have had soup at your apartment," said Cotton.

"No, it's OK. I guess I'm not in the best mood to celebrate. Probably won't be for the next few weeks. You know, morning sickness."

"Oh, yes, of course," muttered Cotton. He tried to sound sympathetic. He realized that a pregnancy was not always going to be a celebratory event. He felt awkward to be gulping down food while watching her fork through her meal.

They finally decided to order containers to take the food home. It was a wise decision because Cotton thought that Jen was looking pale. He helped her into the car and drove the short distance back to her apartment. He double parked in front of her building, put his emergency lights on and helped her up the stairs to her walk up. He got her situated on her coach, retrieved some blankets from a basket near the fireplace and went back to park the car. When he returned, he found her, eyes closed, softly breathing. He decided to camp out in front of her on the floor and listen to the early news. He retrieved a novel on Andrew Jackson that he kept at Jens's house and settled in. At bedtime, he helped her upstairs to her bed and then went downstairs to the couch. He wanted her to get a good night's sleep undisturbed.

He spread the guest sheets out on the couch and fumbled around in the closet for a pillow. He was a little bit too big, but he settled in the best he could. He drifted off to sleep dreaming of nursery rhymes.

Chapter 7

February 6

Cotton woke up at 6:30 the next day, stiff from attaching his 6-3 length onto a piece of furniture that was more love seat than couch. He heard Jen moving around upstairs and went to check on whether she could hold down any food.

"Some toast would be good," she answered from the shower.

He found some wheat bread and bagels and decided that the smell of scrambled eggs might send her off the deep end. She came down with hair combed and a touch of make-up on a face that was paler than usual. Upon sitting down, she rested her head on the table.

"This is one part of being pregnant that is starting to be unbearable."

"Do you have classes today?" asked Cotton.

"Not until this afternoon, thank God," she said. "By then my stomach usually calms down."

"Is there anything I can do for you?" he asked.

"Not right now, but there are always ways that you can pamper me – cook meals, rub my feet, pick up my messes."

Cotton knew that Jen was exaggerating. There were

never any messes to pick up. She was an obsessive housekeeper.

Cotton kissed Jen good-bye and promised to check in during the day on how she was feeling. As he left the house, he had a gnawing feeling that he was abandoning her in her hour of need, but this feeling was overcome by the realization that she was an independent, self-assured woman who could take care of herself.... And the baby... and the baby.

He made the short trip back to his apartment, through an occasional slide on the icy roads. The snow had stopped, and the sun was breaking through a stubborn fleet of clouds. The air was cold, and the chill was bracing. He unlocked the door and brushed aside a pile of mail that had been deposited under the mail slot.

He dropped his brief case and headed straight for the shower, discarding clothes as he went. After a brisk, hot shower, he made his way to his bedroom where he donned a pair of jeans and a sweatshirt. He proceeded to the kitchen where he continued with breakfast – the leftovers of a two-day old pizza. He opened his briefcase and pulled out copies of this week's plans.

Cotton was a tall angular man. He was south Buffalo Irish, with a sprinkling of freckles and a florid complexion that easily turned red whenever he was flustered. He was graceful in his gait and never seemed to gain weight no matter how much he ate. He was a veteran of the Korean War who afterwards went straight into the Buffalo Police department who were giving preference to veterans. He spent two years on the beat before being promoted to detective. He had an enviable clearance rate and was considered a rising star in the department. All this time, he was taking history courses at night at UB. Finding he liked the academic life; he continued working on his master's and finally a PhD. He took a temporary leave from the police to finish us his doctoral work and was pleasantly surprised when UB offered him a position in the history department. By this time, the choice was obvious. He took the position and left the Buffalo Police far behind. Or so he thought....

Jen's path was far different. Raised in New Jersey, she was on an academic path her whole life. Raised by a mother who taught at Rutgers in sociology and a father who was in the history department at Princeton, she was surrounded by academics. She graduated from Columbia with a PhD in history and taught at some prestigious mid-western schools before settling at UB. She was a petite, pert blond with plenty of enthusiasm. She was a favorite of all her students.

Like Jen, Cotton didn't have class until the afternoon, and the subject- the Constitution – was a favorite. He believed that the Constitution was a living breathing document that adjusted to the times. Twentieth century America was not the same as the late 18th century. And the twentieth century America that Cotton and the University were dealing with was certainly not the stuff of Washington and Jefferson.

He worked through mid-day, picking at food along the way instead of sitting down. Half his meals, he realized were eaten standing over the kitchen sink. That would have to change if he was going to live with Jen.

His short drive over to UB was always shorter than his attempt to find a parking place. He was lucky today, only five minutes and he was on his way to his office bundled up against the winter chill.

He was waylaid by a group of students – mostly SDS- who were marching against the war and chanting loudly. The mist from their breath was carried away by a strong breeze.

"Hey, hey, LBJ, how many boys did you kill today?"

SDS, Students for Democratic Society, originated as an offshoot of the socialist group, the League for Industrial Democracy. LID was descended from the Intercollegiate Socialist Society founded by Upton Sinclair, Jack London, Walter Lippman and Clarence Darrow. In 1960 LID morphed into SDS, Students for a Democratic Society. Their first meeting was held at the University of Michigan where Alan Haber was elected President. A manifesto, The Port Huron Statement, was adopted at their first convention in 1962. The manifesto was written by a staff member, Tom Hayden, who would become one of the leaders of the movement. The document promoted participatory democracy and heralded the University as the most logical vehicle to promote their ideas.

Cotton was sympathetic to many of SDS's ideas but was troubled by their increasingly violent means. Having had many in his classes, he knew them personally and allowed them a certain amount of freedom to express their thoughts but, often had to curtail their outbursts which many times had turned into long winded diatribes that kept other students from expressing ideas.

In his office, he began by trying to establish some sense of order to the piles of papers, both research and student, which were growing like some sort of malignant appendage to the chairs and tables that surrounded him. He opened the window to clear the air which he often did regardless of the time of year. He gazed out over the snow-covered commons and the mounds of snow which surrounded the sidewalks like snow sculptures. Even though they were bordering on adulthood, he saw students armed with snowballs hiding behind the snow mounds ready to attack an unaware passerby.

Myerson had lightened Cotton's load because of his responsibilities as a liaison to the student body. Regan had given Cotton a full load probably thinking that if he could bury Cotton with academic responsibilities, he would be less likely to stick his nose where it didn't belong. Cotton had four classes, two being survey courses in American History, one on the Progressive Movement, which he really prized and the other a European course. He loved the Progressive Movement because he could dig deep into the material. The survey courses were so broad that he had little time to examine the material in depth. World War II in one 1/1/2-hour class? He found out that he had to pick and choose which areas he was going to emphasize. He remembered that in high school, the football coach taught history and he spent an endless amount of time on different wars that the United States had engaged in. The size of a cannon, lists of munitions and the number of causalities were lectured upon over and over. Cotton vowed that he would never dwell on conflicts, but instead would deal with issues that led to these events and the people behind these issues. He often spoke of common people and minority contributors to America's growth.

On his way to class, he was waylaid by a skinny Black man dressed in a white lab coat. He introduced himself as Lavelle Hughes and Cotton recognized the chemistry teacher who he had served with on more than one committee.

"Dr. Cunningham, do you have a moment?"

"Lavelle, I'm right on my way to class, but I'll be free at lunch time if that fits your schedule."

"That would be fine. Where do you suggest?" Lavelle asked.

"Norton Hall would be fine with me," Cotton replied.

"I'll be there. Let's say noon?" he asked.

Cotton nodded in assent and then continued down the hall wondering what Hughes wanted to speak to him about. Judging by Lavelle's manner, he could guess. The man had been shaking and his voice quivering when he asked to meet with Cotton. Had something else developed that made Lavelle so nervous? Cotton thought about that on his way to his History 1540 class. He also thought about Regan's admonishment to stay away from any matter that was a police concern.

Could he do that he asked himself? Was he just a teacher now? How much had the events of the past few years made him yearn for the adventure of his days with Buffalo Police Department? All these questions were on his mind that only when he walked into the classroom, set down his materials and faced the class over his lectern did he realized that he was in the wrong room facing a sea of amused faces. Red in the face, he quietly scooped up his papers and backed out to more than a few chuckles.

AFTER class, he hurried back to his office, dropped his materials, grabbed his coat and hat, and proceeded to the Union. Lavelle was waiting at a table that was being cleaned off by an undergraduate student in white garb who was working off his tuition.

"Shall we order first?" asked Cotton.

"I'm just getting coffee," Lavelle said. "I'm too nervous to eat."

Cotton could notice some of the same issues that he had seen in the hallway. His eyes had deep circles underneath, the left one having a pronounced twitch. He was gulping air even though he had been standing still for quite a while.

"Lavelle, what's the matter?" asked Cotton anxiously.

"They're messing with my stuff, man, they're messing with my stuff!"

Cotton could tell that Lavelle was on the edge, near to a breakdown. He needed to do something to calm him down.

"Lavelle, slow down. Tell me what's happened."

Hughes took to out a handkerchief and wiped his brow.

"I don't know if you heard about the chemicals in my lab being switched around?" he asked.

"Yes, Jefferson Drew told me about it." Cotton said.

"Well, it's gotten worse. I lock my lab every night when I leave. The only people who have a key are me and security. A few times I have entered in the morning and found things rearranged. I set up experiments for my first class at 9:00 and things had been altered, not in the student's setup but on my lab desk. A very subtle change – a different powder in a vial. If I had poured the solution I had planned into the vial, it could have caused a small explosion and a subsequent fire. It wouldn't have hurt a student, but would have injured me, probably seriously."

"Have you reported this to security?" asked Cotton.

"Yes, the first thing this morning. They've shut down the lab and we examined all materials to make sure that something else hasn't been tampered with. We'll probably open it up for tomorrow's classes. President Regan has been notified and he's meeting with Drew and me this afternoon."

"Lavelle, there's not much I can help you with. Security is your best bet. I'm sure they will register an incident report with the Buffalo Police. They'll come down and check things out."

"I was told that you were instrumental in solving more than one criminal incident at the college. You used your experience as a former police officer to solve the matters," Lavelle said.

"I've met with President Regan and he let me know that although he wants me to continue to act as a liaison, he doesn't want me to be involved in any police matters," said Cotton.

Hughes seemed crestfallen. "I don't know who to turn to. I feel like security and the police will look upon this as some student prank and dismiss it. A chemistry lab is not like your regular classroom. Some of the compounds can be very dangerous."

Cotton thought for a moment. "I'll tell you what. I'll talk to Drew and see if we can come to some conclusions," said Cotton.

Hughes walked away still not satisfied, but at least aware that he was being listened to. Cotton got another coffee to go and headed back to his office where the endless stream of paperwork awaited. First, he needed to check in on Jen at her office.

"Hey, you. How do you feel?" he asked as he leaned into her workspace.

Her office was like her apartment. Books lined according to size, papers stacked neatly on her desk, sharpened pencils in a wooden box, a comfortable sofa with an Afghan draped over it, a rocking chair set close to an open window. Right now, she was in a comfortable stuffed chair with her feet up on an embroidered divan.

"You mean after throwing up this morning?"

"I'm sorry. Is there anything I can do to help?" asked Cotton.

"Yes. Teach all my classes, clean my house, go to all my committee meetings, push on with my scholarly articles, one which is overdue. You know how most institutions feel about pregnancy, don't you? When I'm pregnant, I can't contribute as much, when I take a leave to deliver, I'm neglecting my duties. Who's going to teach my classes, advise my students? It's not just feeling sick, Cotton, it's the pressure put on me by the college."

"Who's putting pressure on you?" said Cotton, balling his fists.

"It's not one person, it's an atmosphere, offhand comments, and such. I tell you one thing; this college does not promote women taking time off from their jobs unless it's a sabbatical to do research."

"I can talk to the chair, arrange for me to take some of your classes. I'm sure some of our friends in the department will help."

"I know that you can help, but the general feeling is that I'm neglecting my duties. Someday, women will be able to take a maternity leave with benefits and maybe there can be a paternity leave where the father can take time off without a stigma attached."

"I've got quite a few personal days accrued. I can use them to be there right before and after you deliver," said Cotton.

They both paused for a moment in thought. "By the way," asked Jen. "Have you given any thought to a name?"

Cotton was glad to change the topic to a more pleasant one.

"I've tossed around a few names, nothing serious though," he said.

"Come on Cunningham, cough up," Jen said.

"How about Abraham or Theodore?

"My god, Cunningham, I can tell you're a history teacher. Abraham? Abraham Cunningham?

"Well," he said. "Abe Cunningham sounds good."

"What about a girl?" she asked.

"Well, I haven't thought of that. What about you?" he asked.

"I've got about a thousand, but just a few serious ones. Abagail, Dolly….

Cotton broke out laughing over the reference to the names of some of the more famous first ladies.

"No, seriously," he said. "What are a few names?"

"How about Susan, that's my grandmother's name. Or Annette, Grace and for a far out one, Sibyl."

"Sibyl sounds Puritan," he replied. "Back we go to history."

Chapter 8

The Coach

Cotton was sitting in his office when he heard a knock on his door. A tall, handsome man dressed in UB sweats with distinguished salt and pepper hair stood in the entrance way.

"May I come in?" he asked.

"Of course, Dr. Serfustini," said Cotton. UB's basketball coach took a chair and settled in.

Dr. Len Serfustini was a basketball icon in the Buffalo area. He gained fame as a member of the national champion Butler Mitchel's Boy's club in 1942. He played football, tennis and basketball at UB in the late 1940's. After graduation, he later was an assistant basketball coach while achieving his master's in education. He then went to achieve success at Troy State in Alabama where he was NAIA football coach of the year in 1954.

He returned to UB to earn his doctorate in education and took over as UB varsity basketball coach. In fifteen years, he guided the Bulls to six NCAA tournaments. Not only did he achieve success as a coach but was active with several community organizations and was the recipient of many awards. It wouldn't be far off the mark to say he was one of the most respected men in the city of Buffalo.

"What can I do for you?" Cotton asked.

"For one, you can stop meddling in the affairs of the UB basketball team."

Cotton was taken aback by the candid nature of Serfustini's request.

"What do you mean?" asked Cotton although he was fully aware of the basis of coach's remark.

"You talked with Bob Williams about the Black's position on the team."

"He came into my office and stated his case. He asked for my help, and I told him I would investigate the matter with the president. That's my job as a liaison between administration and student." stated Cotton.

"That's what I mean. I got a call from Regan and that started it all. I hope that you won't be carrying this any further."

Cotton was starting to get annoyed. Legend or not, Serfustini was out of line.

"As of right now, I don't anticipate I will be acting on the matter. I'm awaiting any directives from the president."

"Cunningham, I have recruited Blacks on my team before many schools would touch the issue. Way before the Southern schools. I'm not the villain here."

"Then why is William's complaining?"

"Williams wants control. He wants to dictate policy. He wants a voice in hiring and firing. I've never had a player demand that."

"Are the Blacks treated the same as the White players?

"Yes, and in fact we probably bend over backwards considering the political climate in the country."

"What are the chances of hiring a Black coach, someone that they can relate to?"

"Unless I retire, that's not possible. If I retire, then the next coach will probably be from within and then a Black coach hire would be possible."

"Word around town is that your retirement is imminent."

"Until the word comes from me, it's not final."

"Well until I get word from the president, I'm not acting on anything."

"Fair enough," said Serfustini.

They rose and shook hands and the coach departed.

Cotton was glad the way it turned out. He didn't need any more problems on his docket. He had enough as it was. Still the problem remained. How much should he involve himself in the minority assaults? That question was soon to get more complicated.

Chapter 9

February 8

Cotton was in his office when the phone rang.

"Hello," he said balancing a cup of coffee.

"Hello, Dr. Cunningham?" It was a female voice.

"Yes, it is," he replied.

"We've never met, but my name is Connie Parker. My husband Jesse died in an auto accident a month ago."

"Mrs. Parker, I didn't know Jesse but from what I heard he would have been an exceptional addition to our faculty. My deepest condolences to you. Is there anything I can do for you?"

"Dr. Cunningham, I have heard you have helped the police solve several incidents on campus in the past. I wonder if I could meet with you to discuss my situation?"

Cotton immediately remembered Regan's admonition. However, what damage would be done by listening to a grieving widow?

"Of course, we could meet. Where would you suggest?"

"The Eagle House is convenient to me. Do you know where it is?"

"Yes, I do, "said Cotton. "I'm done with classes at 2:30. How about 3:00?"

"Thank you for being available at such a short notice,"

she said and then hung up the phone.

The Eagle House was Erie County's oldest restaurant and once served as a stop on the Underground Railroad. It opened in 1827 and it carried the ambiance of another era. It was still early in the day and finding Connie Parker was no problem. She rose when he entered the dining room.

Connie Parker was a slender woman who was stylishly dressed in a plaid pleated skirt and a plain black turtleneck. Her hair was not styled in the new fashionable Afro but in a straight style of the fifties. He guessed she was in her mid-thirties but her the lines around her eyes and her sober manner spoke to her recent tragedy.

They sat an ordered coffee.

"How are you making do?" Cotton asked.

She took a long time to get her words out.

"I'm keeping busy packing up the apartment. I have a sister in Atlanta, and I'll be staying with her until I get my life back together. I don't know how long that will take."

"How can I help you?" Cotton asked.

She paused again, not knowing how to begin.

"It's about Jesse's death. The medical report indicated that he had a psychotic dose in his body when died. Dr. Cunningham, he was as straight as an arrow, never took any drugs. He had an occasional drink but not before a class. He was drugged and I want to know how and why."

"What did the police say?" asked Cotton.

"They thought he wasn't paying attention to where he was driving, maybe fumbled with his coffee and pastry, but….

"What are you thinking?"

"They didn't say it, but I got the impression that they thought he was a Black man who abused drugs and got what he bargained for."

"Mrs. Parker….

"Connie," she said.

"Connie, the administration of the College has made it clear that they do not want me involved in any police matters on campus. I'm afraid I can't help you. My advice is to keep in contact with the Buffalo Police."

"The Buffalo Police have closed the case, Dr. Cunningham. I need someone apart from the police. Someone who knows their ways but isn't part of their bureaucracy. I need someone like you."

Chapter 10

The Albright Knox Art Gallery

Alberto DiVincenzo was a Purple Heart recipient who fought in the Battle of the Bulge in World War II, headed a battalion during the Korean War and would have fought in Vietnam except for the fact that he was almost a generation too old. He was also an art aficionado.

When Cotton met the Buffalo police detective at the Albright Knox Art Gallery, he marveled at how Alberto could have been the soldier who received all the accolades that he did. He was no taller than five and a half feet and probably weighed no more than 140 pounds soaking wet. He had, however, a commanding voice, an intimidating swagger, and a brash habit of shaking his finger to make a point. When Cotton asked to meet to discuss the minority faculty incidents, Alberto suggested the art gallery as a place that would be innocuous enough and wouldn't attract any attention. Cotton thought that Alberto just wanted someone to lecture at.

The Albright Knox Art Gallery was established in 1905. Its origin was tied to the Buffalo Fine Arts Academy which was founded in 1862 and was one of the oldest public arts institutions in the United States. It is widely recognized as one of the finest modern art museums in the country.

"The Albright Knox is currently featuring the artwork of sculptor James Rosati," said Alberto in his usual basso profundo. "There is also an exhibit on Modular Painting featuring the work of eight young artists. Of course, there are the usual exhibits of Van Gogh, Rembrandt, and Vermeer."

"I'm just interested in the nudes," Cotton said.

He looked back at Cotton with a none too friendly gaze.

"Just joking, just joking," Cotton said.

"While we're touring the museum, you can ask me about these campus incidents," said Alberto.

I proceeded to go through the minority incidents.

"The most serious incident was Jesse Parker. Both Jefferson Drew and I thought it could be murder."

"That one I perused more closely. They found drugs in his system. The drugs were obviously the cause of his accident. A psychotic dose is what they call it. They couldn't pinpoint the exact drug, but they guessed that it might be hallucinogenic."

"Yes, that's what his wife was told. She thinks it was a slap against her husband's good name. She said he never used drugs. And if he did, wouldn't that be an odd time of day to indulge – in the morning, just before class?"

Alberto just shrugged his shoulders. "I didn't know the man. But I could see her objection. A black man using drugs would be a simple solution to the problem. Cops like simple solutions. Close the book and on to the next problem."

"Lavelle Hughes thinks that someone messed his chemicals on purpose and the result could have been a dangerous combination."

"We interviewed Hughes more than once and the guy

was a bundle of nerves. Is it possible that he mixed up the chemicals himself? You know, been in a hurry and inadvertently made a mistake?"

Cotton thought back on Hughes. Alberto was right. He was jittery. But Hughes said it happened twice. What were the odds that he would make the same mistake twice?

"We talked to Jefferson Drew about the incident. He was one of the first on the scene and he related that Hughes was off the wall."

"How did the police settle the matter?" asked Cotton.

"We all agreed, that is Drew and the Buffalo police, that Drew would monitor the situation and that Hughes would double check his chemicals and make sure that his doors were locked."

"But if the doors were locked, as he claimed in the deposition, how could someone have entered the lab?"

"Beats me," said Alberto.

"That leaves the question of Greg Barton being almost run over on campus."

"We questioned Barton. Being a cop, he knows the deal. Just because someone wasn't watching where they were driving and Barton not watching where he was going, doesn't mean attempted homicide. However, Barton swears that wasn't the case. He claims it was a deliberate attempt to run him over. He claims he was watching where he was going, and the car deliberately swerved towards him."

"And Winston Scales?"

"Winston Scales was in the wrong place at the wrong time. A back alley in Allentown? He was lucky he got off that easy."

"Scales didn't think he got off easy. He was roughed up pretty good. He claims he was targeted."

"I don't know how he could think that," said Roberto.

"Still, don't you think that this is too big a coincidence? Four minority members of the campus community are attacked in a short period of time. What are the odds?"

"Slim to none and slim is on vacation. Now let me continue our tour with an examination of these paintings of Jackson Pollock...

Chapter 11

February 9th

Cotton was passing *Your Host Diner* when he spotted a patrol car and saw Greg Barton drinking coffee in the front window.

Greg Barton was Jackson Drew's right-hand man on the security force. A graduate of Cleveland State with a degree in Criminology, he rose quickly in the ranks and transferred over from Cleveland Police to Buffalo Security. He had citation and merit badges all the way up and Drew was glad to have him on the force. He got along well with the student body and had connections with several Black organizations on campus.

Cotton made a short right-hand turn, pulled into a driveway, backed out and turned left to get to a fortunate parking spot.

He entered and grabbed a coffee from the ever-present pot available on a warm - up tray on the counter. He wandered over to the empty seat next to Barton and asked, "Do you mind some company?"

Barton glanced up, his eyes behind Oakley wrap arounds. His outfit was crisp and clean, no small feat in the slush and dirt that the winter produces. It took him a few seconds to recognize Cotton, but soon put his right hand out in a sweeping gesture.

Cotton sat down and sipped his coffee He wasn't ready to have this conversation, but found the time, in private, to be opportune.

"I'd like to ask your opinion on a few things, since you're involved. I've been approached by some people involved in the tragic incidents to minority faculty members. They asked me to help them because their complaints seem to be stonewalled. You probably know that President Regan has asked me not to be involved with criminal matters on campus. Since you were almost run over, I figured you might have some serious opinions on all this."

Barton paused for a moment, glanced down at his coffee.

"I don't have much to add to what you already know. I was stepping off a curb on campus and was lucky that I was looking up. I jumped back just in time. The vehicle even jumped the curb which led me to believe he was aiming for me."

"What kind of vehicle?" asked Cotton.

"I guess you are investigating," said Barton.

Cotton smiled. "People are coming up to me, asking for my help. I'm not trying to overstep my boundaries here. It's your case."

"You're right, it is. I'm sure you've talked to Drew about it. I know you're busy with all the other incidents you've been involved with. Watch out, though. Regan isn't Meyerson. There's trouble brewing, not just on this campus, but all over the country. It will only take one match and this country will burn."

Barton slid off his chair and faced Cotton.

"All I know is that someone tried to kill me, and I want to know why. And it was a beat to shit Chevy that tried to run me over. Probably over a hundred of those on campus. Hard to trace."

"Thanks for the information, I hope you get a solid lead on that car."

Barton tipped his hat and exited into the snowy day.

Cotton thought that even if he were dressed in civilian clothes, people could tell he was a cop. He had that swagger about him, almost an aura of invincibility that was hard to disguise. A good cop, Cotton thought, with a tough outer shell.

Cotton left the *Your Host* soon after. He was behind in his class prep due to trying to take care of Jen and the intrusion of these minority cases. He made his way to his office where he tried to put these other matters out of his mind.

Hours later, the phone rang. Cotton had fallen asleep with his head on his desk. Darkness has fallen and the only illumination was a small corner lamp

He fumbled with the phone and finally put it to his ear.

"Hello, Cunningham here."

There was silence on the other end.

"Hello, who is this?"

More silence. Then two words.

"End it."

And then a click and the call was over.

Cotton, still confused after being awakened out of the blue, was not sure of what he had heard. "End it?" What did that mean? End what? Did it have anything to do with the attempts on minority faculty? Was Cotton going too far?

He stood, fumbled with some books, ran a comb through his hair, pulled on his Navy pea coat and made his way out of his office into the corridor beyond. The area was deserted and illuminated only by an occasional emergency light and the lights of another professor's office.

Normally, an evening walk through the deserted corridors of Diefendorf Hall would not unnerve him, but the ominous phone call put him on edge. Each turn in the hall or stairwell made him apprehensive. He was glad when he finally made it out into the parking lot. The afternoon snowstorm had turned into a rainy drizzle and the slush soon collected in his dessert boots.

He pulled out of a now deserted parking lot. During the day, there was a constant stream of what the students called "parking vultures", cars that tooled around the lots looking for someone who hinted that they may be pulling out of a space. At eight o'clock at night, this wasn't an issue.

He decided that he would stop off at Jen's apartment to see if she needed anything. As luck would have it, there was a spot right in front of her building, the "money spot," as she referred to it. Cotton made it up the dimly lit stairs to her door and let himself in with his own key.

Upon entering, he stopped for a moment. All the lights were off which was unusual. Jen usually lit up the apartment, so much so that he had nick named her Mrs. Edison. At first, he floundered around, with only the lights from the streetlights outside guiding him. He finally made it to a table lamp and pulled the chain. Everything was as it should be - Jen was notorious for her neatness – magazines fanned across the coffee table, Afghans folded neatly across the top of the sofa, counter tops free of any dishes or food, but still no Jen.

Suddenly, there was a voice from the top of the stairs.
"Whose there? Cotton?"

"It's just me, Babe. Are you all, right?

"Yes," she replied with a reassured tone to her voice. "I must have fallen asleep when it was light out. I just woke up and I was totally disoriented. When I heard the noise downstairs, I freaked out."

"I didn't mean to scare you. All the lights were out and that's not like you," said Cotton.

Jen moved into the light and Cotton could see that beside a bad case of hat hair, her complexion was white and her hands trembled.

"Let's get you settled in on the coach and I'll make something for you to eat," he said.

"Nothing too spicy, just keep it bland," she said as she lowered herself onto the couch and pulled the blanket over her.

"How about some soup?" asked Cotton.

"There's some in the cupboard. I'll have the chicken noodle. You can have your choice of the rest."

Cotton chose the hearty meatball with rice variety. After the soups were heated and spooned into bowls, he settled next to her to share the news of the day.

"Not much on my end," said Cotton," Just correcting papers. It was so dark that I must have fallen asleep around 4:00. I was awakened up by the strangest phone call."

"What do you mean strange?" asked Jen.

"Just two words," said Cotton. "End it."

"End it?" what could that mean?" she asked.

"Well, first, I was half asleep when I picked up the phone and the just two words and the caller hung up. It took me awhile to realize that I had a phone call. I'm still trying to process it all."

"And…. Have you figured it out?"

"Well, "end it" could mean quit nosing around this business with the attacks on various members of our minority community."

"Cotton, I was meaning to talk with you about that. I know that you've been talking to Connie Parker about her husband's death, and you feel an obligation to do something, but don't you think we have enough on our plate right now with the baby coming and your teaching responsibilities? And not to mention Teddy..."

Cotton stifled a groan. Teddy was his sister's Down Syndrome child. She was given an ultimatum by her husband – institutionalize Teddy or he would ask for a divorce. With two other children to take care of and a prospect of keeping the family together, she agreed to look for homes for Teddy. The one that they found was close by – Haywood House and after talking with the director and touring the facility, they agreed to move him.

Teddy had been very uncooperative when he realized what was going to happen. He was close to his sister and reveled in the routine of family life. He took the change hard and spent much of the time staring out the window with a depressed look on his face. He shared a room with another boy who tried to be friendly, but Teddy was not interested. He had lost weight and was not flourishing.

He perked up when Cotton came to visit. When they went on an outing it reminded him of the way things were.

On the next day, Cotton planned to take Teddy sledding at Chestnut Ridge in Orchard Park. It turned out to be a sunny day with temperatures in the high twenties – a perfect day to hit the slopes. Cotton has thrown a toboggan in the back of his car and brought along a couple of cheap plastic sleds from Vidler's and spent the whole afternoon up and down the steep hills. At times, they never made it all the way down, overturning in a flurry of snow, laughing and punching at each other. They ended up in the chalet, drinking hot chocolate and warming up.

"Teddy, how are things going at your new home?"

Immediately his demeanor changed. He looked away.

"Teddy, talk to me."

Teddy turned around looking morose.

"Not home!"

"I know it's not your real home. It must be hard to leave your family."

"Nobody comes. Nobody cares about Teddy."

Cotton knew that his sister did her best to visit, but the responsibilities, her household, two children and a husband, who now demanded a lot of her attention, left her little time. She had pleaded with Cotton to visit on a regular basis, but now that Jen was pregnant, his visits had become irregular. When he did visit, it was always to take him out of the institutional setting and go to someplace special.

One unusual outcome of Teddy's relocation was that he was becoming more vocal. And he voiced his displeasure.

"People mean." he said.

"What do you mean?" asked Cotton.

In replay to this he rolled up his sleeve and showed Cotton red rings around his wrist.

"How did this happen?" asked Cotton, a worried look on his face.

Teddy refused to answer.

On the way into Haywood House, he asked one of the attendants about the marks on Teddy's wrist.

"Oh, that could happen in many ways. He could have

been in a fight with another child and had to be restrained. He who could have refused to come to the cafeteria to eat and had to have been forced to eat and there's always the possibility that he did it to himself to get attention when he had visitors."

Cotton didn't know what to think. He knew from talking to childcare specialists that even the best of places for children like Teddy were not great. He promised Teddy that he would come back soon.

Chapter 12

February 12

Winston Scales was sitting in his office next to President Regan's, his arm still in a sling after the beating he took in an Allentown alley a month before. He had invited Cotton to see him, ostensibly to ask him about any information he might have gathered about the diversity affair.

"I know President Regan has made it clear to you that he doesn't want any interference from you into these so-called diversity instances on campus. I also know that Mrs. Parker has contacted you and Lavelle from Chemistry has done the same. I would be amiss if I didn't repeat that warning, but I'm also interested in anything that you might have found concerning these instances since you talked to the president."

Cotton smiled. He had been warned off, but was still useful.

Scales was a recent hire of Regan's. He had administrative experience at Case Western with a background in law enforcement from the federal government. Some people had thought that it was this experience that had attracted Regan's attention. He needed someone that could help him out on a campus where radical factions were lining up and tensions were boiling. Cotton's past allegiance to Meyerson had pushed him out of that equation.

"I don't have much to add to what you already know," said Cotton.

"It's true that these people have contacted me, but I haven't done any investigating for them."

Cotton had decided to keep the phone call he had received to himself. It was true that between Jen's pregnancy, Teddy' troubles and a healthy course load, he hadn't had much time to investigate those matters.

Scales seemed perplexed. He dropped the formalities. "Come-on, Cunningham. You know more than you're saying. Give it up."

Cotton was amused. It was like the old-time cop banter that existed between brothers on the force.

"Honestly, man, I have been way too busy to extend myself in any direction other than personal relationships and my course load. Sure, these people have talked to me, but I haven't done anything for them. How's your body holding up?"

Scales looked down on his sling. "I'm about ready to get rid of this thing. It was a small fracture. The bruises that I had on my face and ribs bothered me a lot more."

"What were you doing in an alley anyways?" asked Cotton.

"That's a long story and I don't want to get into it. Suffice to say that it won't happen again,"

"Good to hear that," said Cotton. "I guess I'll get going."

"Before you leave, I just want to make one thing clear. Any information that you receive about these instances must be funneled into my office. That's a Presidential directive."

Cotton saluted as he left Scales office.

On the way back to his office Cotton mulled over the conversation he just had with Scales. Obviously, Scales knew little more than Cotton about the diversity matters, but his mugging in Allentown must be of some significance because it meant that he was involved in the matter in some way. Was it just a simple matter of someone having it out for faculty members of color? Or did it go deeper than that.

He made it to his office just in time to take a phone call from Jefferson Drew.

"I hear you've been sticking your nose into places where it shouldn't be," he said with a humorous edge in his voice.

"No way," said Cotton. "I know enough to stay away from these things. Besides, I think what Regan really wants to do is to let Amico run full reins over the campus drug lords."

"I didn't call you to talk about Amico. I want you to come with me tonight to meet someone."

Cotton paused. "This sounds mysterious."

"You'll understand when it happens."

They met that evening, underneath the football stands to the far side of the university. The weather was brisk, with a slight dusting of snow. The wind kicked up as they joined a figure in a UB varsity football jacket. He was wearing jeans and high top Keds. A watch cap covered his head. Two-day's worth of a beard covered his face. His eyes were deep set but in the illumination of the stadium lights, he could detect a vivid blue. The stadium seating blocked out some aspects of the light forming a checkerboard pattern over the three. The student was hopping up and down, either nervous or cold.

"Cotton, this is Jack. Jack, Cotton. Jack's not his real name and you never met him here tonight."

Cotton was impressed. As a detective in the Buffalo Police Department, he had informants and they met in the strangest of places. The Buffalo Zoo, on the Maid of the Mist, underneath the Niagara Falls, at a Bison's game in the home team's locker room, at a house of ill repute on Niagara Street and at various movie theatres including the Palace Burlesque.

"Jack is a paid informant of our security force. He has sat in on meetings of the SDS, and Youth against War and Fascism and has channeled some important information to me. He also has informed me that Mike Amico has more than one informant on campus."

"How do you know that, Jack?" asked Cotton.

Jack smiled and the tone of voice indicated what he thought of Cotton's question.

"You get to know who's a student and not, who belongs there and who doesn't. A lot of it is feeling. A student who never has any textbooks, who never communicates with other students. It shows."

"Jack has some interesting information for us." said Drew.

"Some of the leaders of the groups are talking about confrontations. More than just marching. They want to engage, provoke, and cause a disturbance. They believe it's time to, as they say to, "off the pig."

"Do you believe they will actually carry out their threats?" asked Cotton.

"Hard to say," said Jack. "There are informants on both sides. Mike Amico's informants might be willing to stir the pot."

"Why would they do that?" Cotton asked.

"Don't quote me on this because I don't know if it's true, but Amico wants an excuse to come on campus. He doesn't have much respect for campus security. Once anything happens, if security can't handle it, Regan will call him in."

Cotton looked over at Drew.

"He's right. My security force has limited numbers. I've requested more from both Meyerson and Regan with no result. If a large group of students goes on a rampage, we will be at a distinct disadvantage. Plus, my force doesn't have nearly the training in crowd control that the Erie County Sheriffs have."

"What can I do?" asked Cotton.

"You know some of the leaders of these groups. Talk to them, get a dialogue going. There are a lot of issues floating around that these people feel are being ignored."

"Yea, I know. One of the basketball players came to my office the other day. He wanted my help in getting rid of some of the coaches, including Serfustini."

"Good luck with that. He's an institution around here," said Drew.

"And that's just one issue. There's half a dozen more." said Cotton.

They stood there for a moment shuffling their feet as the storm increased in its intensity. The wind picked up and they realized they were underdressed for the storm that was brewing.

One at a time they left and moved in different directions. Cotton and Drew agreed to meet in Drews office at 10:00 the next day to discuss the matter.

On the way back to his parked car, Cotton mused over

the conversation. Classes, Jen's pregnancy, Teddy, the attacks on faculty – there seemed no end to the problems that he seemed to be dragged into. And with no end in sight.

Chapter 13

February 13

When Cotton walked into Jefferson Drew's office the next day, he was surprised to see Mike Amico sitting in one of Drew's office chairs. Talk about the man…

"Cotton, have a seat. Mike just dropped by to see how things are going on campus. I seem to remember that you and Mike don't need an introduction."

"That's right," said Amico. "Cotton and I worked on the same side for years. Although I didn't always agree with his methods, we both had the same goals in mind."

Cotton nodded. "I was a detective. Mike was too, but he was promoted to form a drug task force. He deserved it. He was a hard worker and didn't mind getting his hands dirty. The difference is in our philosophy. He was a shoot first, ask questions later guy. I 'm a bit more circumspect."

"I guess I should take that as a compliment," said Amico. "What I'm really here for is to see if we can combine out efforts."

"Efforts for what!" asked Cotton.

"Guys, Guys, let's not get testy. Mike, if you want our cooperation, you need to let us know what you want."

Amico leaned back in his chair. He had a smug look

on his face. Formerly, a detective in the Buffalo Police Department, he was now Erie County Sherriff. He was respected, and he had the authority to make things happen. He was former Air Force during World War II. He wasn't impressive physically. He was short, with a receding hairline. He wore heavy black rimmed glasses that rested on a prominent nose.

"I've had plenty of experience dealing with college students," said Amico. "They flock to Delaware Park, across from the Albright-Knox Gallery. They use more than grass. They get high on LSD and other addictive drugs. We had one kid who was so wiped out he thought his car was a monster. They were students at UB. Are you telling me they're not doing that on campus – a public institution?"

"What do you want, Mike?" asked Drew.

"I want student files. I want your approval of my men being on campus in an advisory capacity. I want information."

"That's not going to happen," said Cotton.

"I don't believe I was asking you anything, Cunningham!" Amico started to rise from his chair.

"Easy, guys. I'll take your request to the President and get back to you, Mike."

Amico grudgingly moved to the door. He turned around and then paused.

"You were always a bleeding heart, Cunningham. More concerned with the perpetrator than the victim."

After he left, Cotton sat back down and glared at Drew.

"You could have told me that he was going to be here."

"He just showed up as if he owned the place. In a way it's probably a good thing. Now we know what he's after."

"I'm just worried that he might go to Regan and convince him. He knew he couldn't get anywhere with Meyerson. Regan's different. He believes that if the protests pose a threat to everyday student life or if there is a destruction of property, then he's calling in Amico. In a way, the protesters are playing right into Amico's hands. If this campus blows up, Amico rides in on his white horse to save the day and to strengthen Regan's position in the long run."

"I don't believe that Regan wants that to happen. It would be a black mark on the College while he's President. Everyone would remember who was in charge when it happened."

"Talk to your connections with these groups and after that we'll have to see how it plays out," said Drew.

Cotton left his meeting completely drained of optimism. Waiting for things to play out was not in his DNA.

He wandered back to his office with a short detour to Norton Union to pick up a sandwich for lunch. He was expecting to have lunch in Jen's office, and then spend the rest of the day working on class work that he was sorely neglecting. He had a class at 1:00 and 3:00 and he was looking at a long day.

The weather was surprisingly spring like except for the snow piled high along the sidewalk edge. The sun was resplendent and coated the drab colors of the surrounding buildings like a new paint job. The students, forever optimistic weather wise, were out in shorts equipped with footballs and Frisbees. There was a general air of better things to come. Cotton was all about positive thinking, but he was no February fool. He expected the weather and student activism were only going to get worse, and he felt helpless to turn the tide.

When he got to his office, he found three students waiting and he remembered that he was late for office hours.

"Sorry, guys. I'll take you one at a time. I promise not to keep you waiting too long." He dropped his brief case by his desk and ushered the first student in. Ralph Richards was a junior from Montauk, Long Island. He was enthusiastic in class, always with his hand raised to contribute to the conversations. The only drawback was that students like Ralph tended to dominate the conversation and Cotton always was on the lookout to get the less talkative students involved. It was an innocuous conversation concerning credit hours and what he needed to graduate on time the following year.

The next student was Lenore Wilkinson, a sophomore from Grand Island New York. She was interested in clearing up an issue with the syllabus. She was the kind of student who was paranoid about due dates. Although Cotton made these things very explicit, she needed reassurance.

The final student was Elroy Benson. Cotton was glad to see him. He was a member of SDS, and even though he was there about an academic matter, after that was settled, Cotton wanted to question him about what the SDS had planned. After he had answered his questions about an extension on a paper due that week, he found an opportune time to question him about SDS.

"So, have anything planned in the near future?"

Elroy smiled. "Man, you know better than me, take for example, the issue of blacks on the basketball team All they want is a Black coach at some level – it doesn't have to be a head coach. Just someone who would listen to them. Do you think Surf's going to listen to some poor Black kid fresh out of the ghetto? No, he has other things to think about. Project Themis is another issue. Why would the campus align itself with the Department of Defense at a time when we're fighting an unjust war in Asia? There are things on a national level that concern us and they only way we can get our voices heard is with on campus protests Sure we know that Regan and other administrators aren't responsible for the war, but we work with what we've got. I can't take off and spend months protesting outside the Pentagon or the White House. I must graduate and on time. But we sure can raise hell on this campus and if enough campuses do the same then our voices might be heard."

Cotton thought his argument made sense. But there was one drawback.

"But what if it leads to violence? What if someone gets hurt?"

Elroy shrugged his shoulders. "How many kids my age, little snot nosed boys just past their senior prom come back in coffins? And we should be afraid of being pushed around by a bunch of cops. No, Professor, what we can give is a small price to pay."

Cotton didn't realize that it was past lunchtime until he looked at his watch. He shut the door to his office and hurried over to meet Jen for lunch. When he arrived at her office her door was shut and there was a note on her door.

Professor Valley has canceled all her classes for today. She asks that you continue work on your projects and follow the syllabus for next class.

COTTON panicked. He hurried to the department secretary. "Did you take a call from Jen?"

"Yes, I did, Cotton and she told me to assure you that there was nothing seriously wrong and that you shouldn't go running out of the building. full tilt. She's just feeling like shit, and she wanted to go back to bed."

"And Cotton, some advice. Pregnant women occasionally feel like shit and sometimes just want to be left alone. Take my advice, give her the day. Go about your business and keep to your schedule. Don't go running off to rescue her. She's a very independent woman. She doesn't need fawning over."

Cotton smiled. "Sounds like she's been confiding in you. I can take a hint."

He returned to his office to grade papers. He glanced over at his phone, but decided he didn't. want to wake her up if she was napping.

He spent the rest of the afternoon correcting papers and going over projects that were due the next week. He was balancing his workload with his private life, but he was determined not to let his classes suffer. Most of the students in his survey courses were inquisitive students and independent learners, but there were a few who needed individual guidance and he wanted to be sure that he was available.

He took a call around 3:00 from the President's secretary asking if he was available to meet with him in an hour. Even though it was a request, it was accepted that one did not turn down such an invitation. He assured her that he would be there.

He made it to Regan's office ahead of time. The secretary was gone for the day, but his office was open. He heard voices from inside, so he lowered himself into a chair to wait.

In a few minutes, Jefferson Drew emerged from the office and walked past him with a look that said, "It's your turn."

Regan appeared at the office door and motioned for

Cotton to follow him in. There was no offer of coffee this time and Regan got right down to business.

"I just spoke to Jefferson Drew just now and Greg Barton earlier in the day. Also, Mike Amico by phone at lunch time. It seems that my request for you to stay out of police business has fallen on deaf ears. Could you explain to me why you are ignoring my directive?"

Cotton was completely caught off guard. He scrambled to reply.

"I have not gone out of my way to investigate any matters that are better off handled by the police. People have come to me and asked for my assistance. I have relayed your feelings to them about my position on such matters. I have not actively done any investigating into their requests. Things just keep on falling into my lap. I assure you that I have enough going on in my life that I don't have to spend my time doing police work."

This seemed to temporarily mollify Regan.

"I will take your word on that Cunningham and Drew assured me that you will be working with some members of the radical student body to stem any violence or destruction of property that their demonstrations might cause."

"I am in the process of doing just that. However, there is another matter that I would like to speak to you about. I worked with Mike Amico for many years when I was on the Buffalo Police Force. He was the head of their narcotics division and is very aggressive in his job. The problem is that he believes that UB students are some of the main drug dealers in the city. He has a very low opinion of our students. He would like nothing better than to have an open door to police this campus. I think that would be disastrous. I don't think he can be trusted to have the best interests of the college at heart."

"Well, Cunningham, he didn't have anything good to say about you in the phone call that I took this morning. Said you were soft as far as the students were concerned and that you were, in his words, "a lousy detective "who cared more about the accused than the victim."

"Funny, those were just the words he used when we talked earlier this morning."

"Regardless, no matter who comes to you and asks for your help, do not engage in any matters above your pay grade. You're a teacher first and a conduit to the student population. Do I make myself clear?

"I hear you, Sir."

Cotton was in a hurry to get to Jen's apartment. He went directly to his car and drove across town to her walk-up apartment in Allentown. When he entered the apartment he found her on the couch, under a blanket in her night gown.

"I won't ask how you are, but is there anything I can do?"

"She had tears in her eyes. "You know how bad it must be for me to cancel classes. I just feel so crappy that I don't want to get up of the couch. I haven't even dressed for the day. "

Cotton nodded sympathetically. He knew that she just wanted an ear to listen. There was nothing he could say to make her feel any better.

"How was your day?" she asked.

He related to her the meeting with Drew and Amico and finally the command appearance with the President.

"I know how you love Mike Amico," she said. "How did

you work with him when you were with the Buffalo Police?"

"Our paths didn't cross that frequently, but he made the rounds. He was extremely ambitious and very outspoken, and he had the ear of the sheriff. Once he became sheriff last year, he spread his influence everywhere. There isn't a part of the BPD that he isn't familiar with."

"Can't you just avoid him?" she asked.

"He's confrontational and he resents the fact that the College is not part of his fiefdom."

"Is there anything I can get you?" he asked.

"Nothing, just having someone around is a comfort."

They spent the rest of the evening reading and watching television. When Cotton left a little before midnight Jen was asleep on the couch. He let himself out and went back to his apartment.

Chapter 14

February 14

He had a job to do, and Cunningham was getting in the way. He knew that Regan had admonished Cunningham about his interference in police matters. The Buffalo police had given up on the attacks on minority members of the faculty, but he was not to be denied. He had been tasked by the governor to find out who was behind the attacks and why. The governor was sensitive to such matters ever since the inner-city riots.

Drew was not much help. He was worried about student unrest as he should be. The place was a powder keg ready to explode. In his past assignment with the FBI, he had been sent to California to investigate the free speech movement and Mario Savio. Ronald Regan was governor of California at the time, and he took a dim view of student violence.

Were the attacks somehow connected to student unrest on campus? As far as he knew, none of the far-left organizations were racist. In fact, SDS and other radical groups went out of their way to work with Black groups and generally sympathized with their demands.

In his position, he was privy to information about such incidents on campus and he was using that position to investigate the best he could. Perhaps he could use Cunningham without him knowing it. It was worth a try.

Cotton woke up the next day feeling that he should be taking care of Jen. But then he remembered the conversation that he had the day before. She was an independent woman and if she needed help, she would ask for it. He showered and shaved and picked up the house as best as he could. When he was busy, the house suffered. And the bills – he had to pay the bills. Things were piling up on the domestic front that had to be attended to. He took a few hours to get some menial tasks accomplished before he headed out to the college.

It took him several minutes to find a parking space and on the walk across campus he was met with the sound of loud voices chanting in a rhythmic fashion. He was used to it by now. Many of the protesters were active all throughout the day. It was the constant background noise as familiar as the clock striking on top of Hayes Hall.

"Hey professor, come join us. "

"I can't guys. I'm neutral. My job is to teach. I can't take sides. Besides, I don't do well in this type of weather. I get the sniffles."

He made it to his office just in time to correct some papers before his 11:00 class. He was stopped in the hallway by Ned Davis, a janitor who worked days.

"Hey, professor, is someone else sharing your office these days?"

"What do you mean, Ned?"

"Well, early this morning, this guy was unlocking your office door."

"Could it have been maintenance. I've had a few problems with the heating."

"I don't know. I know most of those guys and I didn't recognize him."

"What did he look like?"

"I only saw him from behind. He was. medium height, dark hair and he might have been a Negro or maybe Mexican."

That wasn't a great description in Cotton's mind. It fit quite a few students or faculty. Why would someone be interested in what Cotton had in his office? Did this have anything to do with the minority incidents? A student wanting a test copy? That was absurd. No student would risk breaking into a professor's office for such a reason. The break-in didn't make sense.

Cotton had just settled in when Connie Parker appeared at his office door.

"Dr. Cunningham, I know I should have made an appointment, but I was afraid that you wouldn't see me. Do you have a moment?"

Cotton sighed. "Come in and have a seat."

Mrs. Parker was dressed conservatively in a dark plaid skirt, dress shoes, a black sleeveless sweater over a white shirt. Pearl earrings stood out against her dark skin.

"Mrs. Parker, I know that you have asked for my help, but I have been told more than once by President Regan that I should not involve myself in police matters. I'm getting pressure from above."

"It's not in the hands of the police anymore. They've given up." she said.

"Then I suggest a private detective. I know quite a few from my time on the Buffalo Police Force."

"I'm coming back to you because there is something that I just remembered that might have something to do with his death."

Cotton was silent for a few seconds. Surely, it wouldn't hurt to hear her out.

"O.K., Mrs. Parker, what would that be?"

"He had a feeling, in the weeks before his death, that someone was following him. He mentioned it a few times at dinner. Nothing that he was sure of, just, you know, seeing something out of the corner of his eye, a noise in a parking lot. I think it might have something to do with his accident."

"I've been warned off the case. I don't think that a small suspicion warrants a reexamination of your husband's death."

"But it's not a small suspicion. I feel that it's a definite clue that points to murder, not an accident."

Cotton felt sorry for her. Her life, planned out, career and family, was now ripped apart. He didn't feel like he could just disregard her.

"Is there anything else that you can think off that would lead you to believe that he was murdered?"

"He was uneasy, in the weeks before his death. I don't think it was a premonition, just that he was not himself."

"I still have some friends in the police department. I'll give them a call and see what evidence they have."

"I don't have much faith in them. They think he was a druggie."

She wasn't enthusiastic when she left Cotton's office. Cotton knew he should stay away, but this new bit of information was interesting.

Cotton's class that afternoon dealt with the assassination of William McKinley. He was shot at the Pan American Exposition in Buffalo. In 1901, Buffalo was one of the leading cities in the country. Its position for shipping grain from the Mid-West made it a terminal on the Great Lakes. Teddy Roosevelt was sworn in at the Wilcox mansion on Delaware Avenue. It was the kind of notoriety that Buffalo did not need.

He lectured about Theodore Roosevelt, his youth as an underdeveloped, sickly child, boxing lessons, his early career in New York City politics and his rise to the governorship. His foray on San Juan Hill with the Rough Riders paved the way to the vice presidency.

On his way out of class, he was stopped by a cadre of students who wanted to know about projects that were coming up in the future.

One of the students wanted to know if she could grade herself.

"I have a class in College A across the street and they let us grade ourselves."

College A thought Cotton. There was a catastrophe if he ever saw one.

College A was an experimental college across the street from the main campus. It was part of the reforms that had been established by Martin Meyerson in his first years as President. Some of the classes were bogus, like wood carvings. And then, there was the issue of self-grading.

"No, you can't self-grade, but I will allow you to comment on the grade I put on your project."

The student sulked away.

Some students, members of SDS, gathered around Cotton and quizzed him about the administration's response to the picketing.

"What do they have up their sleeve now?" asked Ned Pulana, a senior from Orchard Park, New York.

"I think they're waiting to see what you propose to do," Cotton said.

The crowd dispersed and Cotton walked back to his office. On the way, he checked his mailbox which was overflowing as usual. He found Greg Barton waiting for him.

"I heard that you might have had a break in at your office this morning?" he said.

"That was quick. I didn't have time to report it," said Cotton.

"Someone called it in. Is there anything missing?"

"I haven't had the time to check. Come on in."

They pushed in through the open door and glanced around. Everything seemed to be in order, although it was hard to tell since Cotton's order was another person's chaos. He glanced about. It seemed to be fine.

"It all seems to be in order, nothing missing as far as I can see."

Barton grunted. His shirt and pants were neatly pressed. Mustache trimmed. If his appearance was any indication, his office must be just the same. "Let me know if you find otherwise," said Barton as he ambled out the office door.

What was that all about thought Cotton? As far as he knew, Ned was the only person that knew about the break-in. News must travel fast around the office.

COTTON was perplexed. Why would anyone want to break into his office? He had nothing of value, only books and mementoes of when he worked for the Buffalo Police. And then again, it could have been a maintenance man checking on the heat. Didn't he complain about it to the secretary back in the fall?

Winter sun was flowing through the window as Cotton eased into his desk chair. He had class work to do but his talk with Mrs. Parker stayed with him. He had been warned off by more than one person, but his sense of duty as a human being, and not just a professor at the college, nagged at him. The attacks were not a coincidence. One or two maybe, but four minority teachers attacked with one death included was a pattern, a pattern that couldn't be ignored. He had already been asked to intercede by two people. What was President Regan doing about it? Was he just referring it to the Buffalo police? Did he have any reason for covering it over? The University, still recovering from incidents of violence in the past two years, didn't need any more disturbances, but covering up the incidents or just ignoring them would not serve the college well. He tried to shake off these questions and return to schoolwork but failed.

Chapter 15

February 16

"Hey, Babe, do you feel well enough to look over a few houses tomorrow?" Cotton and Jen were having a light dinner at Jen's apartment on Friday evening. She was in good spirits having had a couple of days without sickness. She was tired most of the time, which was to be expected, but had expressed a desire to take part in Saturday house hunting.

"I think I can manage it, although I do have tons of classwork to catch up on."

"There're a few houses that I think are worth looking at in the south towns, one in Wanakah."

"What does the ad say?" she asked.

"Two floors, three bedrooms, two upstairs and one downstairs that could be converted into an office, a formal living room and small dining area and kitchen. The garage is attached. Fenced in backyard with small concrete patio. Quiet residential street with paved driveway.

"It sounds like it's worth looking at," she said.

Cotton felt guilty devouring a breakfast of hash browns, scrambled eggs and waffles. Jen stuck with a milder order of toast and coffee. It was overcast and the threat of lake effect snow was keeping most people indoors for the evening.

"How is Teddy doing?" she asked. "I didn't ask you about your last visit."

"Fine when he's out with me and miserable when I take him back to his room. He is having problems adjusting to his roommate. The guy doesn't seem to be bad, but Teddy is used to having his own room. His roommate tries to get him involved in conversation, but that's not Teddy's strongpoint."

"It doesn't seem like there are many options. He'll just have to get used to the group home."

"I know that, but I just hope that someday he'll be able to be in a more family-oriented situation. Group homes can be depressing."

"I know that it bothers you to no end, but I don't see any solution in the near future."

They finished up the meal in silence, washed dishes and went to bed early missing the eleven o'clock news by a long shot.

The next day, they took off early after breakfast, to keep a few real estate appointments. The house in Wanakah was having an open house so they saved that for last.

One house was in Orchard Park and was much too big a house for a couple expecting their first child. Besides, Orchard Park prices were out of sight and would have to wait for one of them to win the lottery. The second house was in Derby and seemed to be too far out for a commute to downtown Buffalo.

The house in Wanakah was intriguing. It was on a side street off a road that meandered from an elementary school situated on Lake Erie to the top of a hill where a new middle school was situated.

"It certainly is a quiet neighborhood, although it might come alive during the summer, "said Cotton.

The front door was open, and they entered the house which was already crowded with two other couples. Cotton didn't mind that. He didn't want someone to be crowing in his ear while he was trying to inspect the premises.

The rooms were small, but cozy. He tried to imagine it with furniture. The living room walls were an off-white color, and a fireplace was situated at one end. The only thing that bothered him was the small bathroom situated on the first floor. There was no master bedroom, just three similar rooms, two upstairs and one down. All the rooms were small except for the living room.

"What do think?" he asked Jen when they were out of earshot of the perky blond real estate agent.

"Nothing stands out as noteworthy, but our needs are simple. A bedroom for us upstairs and one close by for the baby. I do wish that there was a bathroom upstairs. The cellar seems dry and that's a big point with hookups for washer and dryer. Good house to start out with, I think. How about you?"

"The size of the bathroom bothers me. There is room upstairs between the bedrooms to fit in a larger bathroom later. The big selling point is the price. Almost half of what the other houses we saw cost."

Cotton caught up with the woman who was showing the house.

"The price is very affordable. Was someone murdered in the living room?"

The real estate agent didn't seem to appreciate his humor. "The house is a little too far out for some. Most people like the convenience of the large shopping centers. It's a neighborhood that's going to be vibrant in the next ten years. Buy now and when you outgrow it, make a bundle."

As they exited the house, they saw an older woman

next door shoveling out a path to her walkway. She turned towards them with an infectious smile.

"It's a nice house on a quiet street. You wouldn't regret it. That is, unless you have five kids."

"No," said Jen. "Just one on the way. Do you know why the people are selling?"

"Grew out of it. With four kids, they ran out of bedrooms."

They drove back with the little house on Greenfield Avenue on their minds. The ride was in stormy weather with snow pellets raking their windshield and icy conditions moving the car back and forth across the road.

"That's the thing about the South Towns. Lake effect snow slams this area. Let's time the trip back."

They made it into Jen's apartment in 35 minutes – quicker than they expected. When they peeled off their coats and pulled off their boots, Jen noticed the answering machine blinking. She pressed the button to listen.

"This is Jefferson Drew. I've tried to reach Cotton on both his home and office line. I thought perhaps he might be with you, Professor Valley. If he is, tell him to call me on the double. There's trouble brewing on campus."

Cotton called Drew on his office line and got his answering machine. He left a message and decided he better take off for campus. After a good-bye kiss to Jen, he took off down Delaware Avenue. It was a Saturday, so finding a parking space wasn't a problem. The snow was now turning to slush and his wipers were working full time. He entered Drew's office area and found it abandoned. On Drew's secretary's desk was a scrawled note that said for him to meet him in Regan's office upstairs.

Regan's secretary was off for the weekend, but Regan's door was open and bright light flowed from it. Cotton moved to the door and heard an animated conversation from within.

"I think letting Amico on the campus based on a rumor is unadvisable. It could set off a chain reaction that would cause a riot."

"Your informant gave us the information and if it's true then we need to act quickly," said Regan.

They both turned when Cotton entered the room.

"Cotton, maybe you could help us out here." said Drew.

Cotton sat down in one of the president's upholstered guest chairs next to Drew while Regan sat in shirtsleeves behind his desk.

"One of my informants, you met him the other day, passed on some information to me late last night. Basically, he said that SDS was planning to march on this building and take over the offices."

"There's no way that is going to happen. I'm not as conciliatory as Martin was. If there's a chance of that happening, I'm calling Amico in," said Regan.

"Jefferson, what exactly did he tell you about what SDS planned?" asked Cotton.

"He said that they were planning a war council. They thought that the administration was not listening to their requests for change, and they had no other recourse than to force the issue."

"Requests?" snorted Regan. "They were more like demands. Hiring and firing basketball coaches, ending Project Themis, they wanted to have a voice in running the day-to-day operations of the college. Outrageous!"

Regan was pounding on his desk, red faced and trembling.

"President Regan, all I'm asking is that you let us speak

with the leaders of SDS and see if we can talk some sense into them," said Drew.

"Sir, although I just walked into this, I think what Jefferson proposes is the logical way to deal with the problem," said Cotton.

Regan turned in his chair and looked out over the wind-blown snow-covered campus.

"I'll give you two school days to speak with their leaders. By then, I'll need to have some assurance that they won't carry out their threats."

"Thank you, Sir," said Jefferson Drew and Cotton nodded his reply.

"Come with me to my office," said Drew as they passed out of the secretary's office. They continued deep down into the bowels of the office building without a word, as if the hallways would betray them. When they finally reached Drew's office, he ushered Cotton in and then slammed the door shut.

"I don't think he understands what bringing Amico onto this campus would do," Drew said, taking off his jacket and flinging it over a chair.

"A clash like that could be the breaking point on a campus already on the edge. You're right about one thing – he's not Martin."

"I asked you here because you know them on a first name basis. Maybe they'll listen to you."

"I know Kearns and some others, but if I talk to them about a war council, they'll want to know how I got the information. They are already sensitive about informants in their groups. You know, you're not the only one who does that. I'm sure Amico has people on the inside also."

"I'm sure he does and I'm sure that Regan is going to hear from him before long. I'm glad I got to Regan first.

Before the weekend is over, I'm sure that Amico will know that we are going to be talking to SDS. I'm even sure that Amico's snitches are pushing for violent action just to get him and the police on campus."

Cotton and Drew sat in silence for a second.

"I think we're just delaying the inevitable, but I'll talk to these people and see what I can do. I have some in class and they're pushing to turn my classes into forums for their grievances. The most I can hope for is to establish some sort of dialogue with them. I don't know if having them speak to Regan is the answer. He's more of a hot head than some of the SDS people."

"Get them engaged with the vice president in charge of student affairs or maybe someone along those lines," said Drew.

"It's the weekend and I don't know if I can contact them, but I'll try," said Cotton.

"Keep in touch and call me if I can help," said Drew.

Cotton left the building with a weight on his shoulders. To many weights to be sure. He had phone calls to make and meetings to arrange.

Chapter 16

February 17

Cotton knew two students, Terry Keegan and Tom Kearns who were active in SDS and who had been previously registered in his classes. Back at his office, he checked his records to see if he had any phone numbers for the two. No phone numbers, but addresses for both, although he wasn't sure if they were current.

He called Jen, appraised her of the situation, and then went off into the early evening to search for the two students.

Keegan's last address was near Canisius College off Jefferson Avenue. Near a bar that was a favorite of Canisius students called Strinka's, it was a downstairs flat with an enclosed porch that was filled with the detritus of dozens of coming and going college students. Disabled bikes, a broken-down washing machine, discarded Christmas decorations and plug in electric bar signs littered the enclosed area. Cotton pushed through the mess and knocked on a door that was scuffed and dented.

After what seemed to be an eternity, the door was hauled open by a diminutive coed with an Afro and a sweatshirt that proclaimed, "Free Huey." She was barefoot in bell bottoms and smelled faintly of baloney, raw sweat, and hashish.

"Yea?" she said, staring at Cotton through glassy eyes.

"I'm looking for Terry Keegan. This was his last known address."

She starred at Cotton for an endless moment and finally yelled back into the hallway. "Hey, Josh. This guy is looking for Terry Keegan."

Out of the gloom of a dimly lit hallway, emerged an emaciated figure that resembled Nosferatu out of the silent films. He looked Cotton over and replied in a voice that had a touch of an eastern European dialect.

"Keegan no longer resides here. He was in a rush to leave, and we were left holding the bag so to speak. We would like to find out where he lives and recoup our losses."

"If you could give me any information of where he might have gone, I will be sure to pass information back to you if I find him," said Cotton.

"Supposedly, he moved in with his girlfriend, whose last name was Simpson, somewhere by Buffalo State, behind the Art Gallery." he said.

"Thanks," said Cotton.

As he moved off the front porch, he felt the hairs on the back of his neck rise. Off campus student residences, at times, resembled third world habitats.

He drove to a corner phone booth and a number that he knew by heart. The voice that answered was familiar. "Hello."

"Dolores, it's Cotton Cunningham. Remember that wonderful dinner we had at Manny's a couple of years back? It set me back a paycheck, but the pleasure of your company was well worth it."

There was a distinct pause on the phone and then the lilt of laughter.

"Yea, I remember, and I also remember that you never called me back. The first date was the last date. What do you want, Cotton?"

"Cut to the chase, I guess, Dolores." "I'm looking for an address for a woman named Simpson who might be a UB student. Girlfriend to Terry Keegan."

"Keegan, I know. In the past SDS has threatened to shut down the Registrar's office. You're lucky I have my home computer linked to the college."

She returned a few moments later with an address. "Faye Simpson, 52 Edgewood Terrace off Delaware Avenue in North Buffalo."

"Dolores, I owe you one. Perhaps a Norton Hall lunch."

"I won't hold my breath, but it would be cheaper than Manny's, wouldn't it?"

They both laughed.

It took Cotton a little less than 20 minutes to get to the address and was surprised to find it was a neatly kept two story post war split level with an attached garage. There was a VW van parked in the plowed driveway. It was as far away from student housing as you could get. Cotton parked behind the van and walked up to the front door. He lifted a brass knocker and let in drop. In a minute, the door opened, and he faced a fresh-faced young woman in neatly pressed jeans and a red sweater and scarf.

"May I help you?" she asked.

Cotton must have looked astonished because she had to repeat her question.

"I hope so," Cotton replied. "I seem to be in the wrong place. I'm looking for Terry Keegan."

Her smiled continued. "He is sleeping right now. He's very busy as a student and with his co-curricular activities."

"I'm sorry, I haven't introduced myself. My name is Cotton Cunningham. He's one of my students at UB and I needed to discuss something with him."

Her smile vanished. "I'm sure this has nothing to do with academics. He has been victimized by people who misconstrue his intentions."

"Terry is a prime member of SDS. I have been tasked by the president to ask as an intermediary between students and the administration. I have been informed that SDS is going to be very active in the coming weeks. The president wants me to talk to people involved to see if we can keep things peaceful."

There was a rumbling from deeper in the house and Keegan emerged tousle haired and sleepy eyed.

"What's up?" He spied Cunningham and then half scowled, "Dr Cunningham, how did you find me?"

"I checked with the Registrar, and they gave me an address. Also, the people who you lived with before would like to speak to you about past rent."

Keegan turned red and then spoke. "I don't think you found me to just give me that message. What's up?"

Cotton looked over at Keegan's female companion.

"She can hear whatever you have to say," he said.

"The administration got wind of a rumor that SDS is planning something big and disruptive on campus very soon. President Regan tasked me to talk to some SDS leaders and see if I can avert a disaster."

Keegan paused, went back into what must have been a kitchen, returned with an apple and started munching on it while stretching out on a couch with his feet on a table full of magazines.

"It's nice to know that we're finally getting some attention from the powers to be," he said. He was enjoying this.

"I thought we could talk about it and come up with some ideas about communicating issues."

"We've been trying to communicate for a long time, but the administration didn't want to listen. What about the Black students and the coaching situation, the war in Vietnam, the college's participation with the military? Where does the college stand on those issues?"

"The basketball situation is being worked on. I don't know what you want the college to do about that and ROTC is all but dead in the water. I think the college is willing to meet with representatives of all the groups to discuss solutions."

"I think the college is good at saying one thing and doing another. I think they are not serious about any substantial change. I think the only thing that moves them is physical confrontation."

"The only thing that physical confrontation is going to do is to get the Buffalo Sherriff on campus. You know that Amico is dying to see you and others in jail. Is that what you want?"

"If that's what it takes to get their attention, then that's what we'll do", he said defiantly.

"Can I let the president know that you at least talk it over, before you go ahead with what you've got planned?"

"We'll talk. Set a date for this week. I'll be there. Set a time and a place."

"Good. I'll get in touch with you. We have class on Tuesday. I'll let you know then.

He turned to the girl. "This is a very nice house miss."

"My parents are away for the winter. They trust me to take care of the property."

Cotton left thinking that he had accomplished something. Whatever would come out of the talks, he couldn't predict, but at least he had made progress. Perhaps, he was stalling the inevitable, but it was all he could do.

His next move was to call on Tom Kearns, but it would have to wait until Sunday. It was getting late and Cotton wanted to check in with Jen. She was correcting papers when he called from a pay phone.

"I'm doing fine. Just catching up on some paperwork. How did it go with Keegan and Kearns?" she asked.

"I talked with Keegan. He'll meet with representatives of the college. He's not optimistic about the outcome. He says that the college has had enough time to settle their grievances. He thinks that a confrontation is what's needed to effect change."

"That's too bad. I think the whole situation can be resolved, at least partially resolved, without riots in the streets."

"I hope you're right. In the meantime, I have another student to get in contact with."

It did not take long for that to happen. He was in his office on Monday when he received a phone call.

"Dr, Cunningham, this is Tommy Kearns. I hear you're looking for me."

Cotton thought, *Keegan called him.*

"Yes, I am. How are you doing?"

"Let's skip the formalities, professor and talk about what you propose."

"Like I told Keegan, we just want to get together and talk about averting any violence on campus. He agreed to meet with representatives of the college. I hope you'll consider the same."

There was silence on the phone for almost a minute and the Kearns said, "I must talk with some people and get back to you. But don't count on that get together. There are a lot of angry people out there. People who have been ignored for years, not just from the college, but from the community as well."

"I understand and I hope you'll follow up and get back to me in time to avert a tragedy," said Cotton.

There was a pause on the phone.

"Have you ever read *Letter from A Birmingham Jail* by Martin Luther King?"

"You know I have. I used it in your class." Cotton knew where he was going with this.

"In it he said that when they met with Birmingham merchants in negotiations, they said they would remove degrading signs from their store windows. After a few months went by, it was apparent that they had no intention to do that. That was when he argued that direct action was necessary. He said that it proved that they were not moving recklessly into confrontation."

"You always were a smart ass, Kearns."

Kearns chuckled on the other end of the line. "See you at the meeting."

Between correcting papers and preparing for a class on the New Deal, he was busy when Jefferson Drew called.

"Did you make any headway in this mess?"

"I think I did. I talked with both Keegan and Kearns. They weren't optimistic but agreed they would try to get their people to agree on meeting with us before they attempted any confrontation. Now we must set a time and place."

"I talked to Regan, and he won't be at the meeting, but

Vice President Boyle will be there. If you can let them know that the meeting will be at his office on Tuesday at 2:00, that will be settled."

"I think that they would want to speak to Regan. I don't know how they'll feel about that, but I'll let Kearns know today in class."

"How did it go with them?"

"They were obstinate, claiming that the college has ignored them. They claim the only way to get anything done is by confrontation."

"You know, they're probably right. There are some hard liners in the administration that think that the radical population has been placated. Look at College A and what they did to the ROTC offices last October. Regan has made it clear that he thought Martin let the students run the college."

"Regardless, Jefferson, this might be our only chance to let them know that we care about their grievances. I'll let Kearns know."

After class, Cunningham caught Kearns and informed him of the time and place of the meeting.

"On their turf and on their time. They're still calling the shots, eh?"

"It was the best I could do Tommy."

"And what about Regan? Will he be there?"

"I'll talk to him. I'm sure he'll be there at some point."

Kearns left, obviously disappointed but willing to make some phone calls about the meeting.

Barton was waiting for him when he got to his office.

"I hear that there's going to be a meeting with students and administration."

"Do you want to come in and sit down? I hate discussing things like this in hallways."

They entered the room and Cunningham lifted some papers of a chair and beckoned Barton over. Barton stood for a moment, and they slowly eased himself into the chair.

"Yes, we are having a meeting tomorrow at the vice president's office. Did you want to be present?"

"I asked my boss, but he said it would be prudent, those were his words, prudent if I stayed away. Too many cops, I guess."

"He might be right."

"I know some students, especially the Black students, some of whom are involved with the basketball controversy. I think I could bring a different perspective, especially if some of the Black groups are represented at the meeting."

"You might be right," said Cotton. "I'll talk to Drew about it. You might be valuable."

Barton left the office and Cotton wondered whether there were other reasons Barton came to see him.

He dropped in on Jen at her office. She was conferencing with a student. He didn't want to disturb the conversation, so he drifted down to check his mail. The secretary was a substitute and was not so much into conversation as she was into blowing bubbles.

He leafed through his mail, deposited the junk and returned to his office with two pieces of correspondence. One was a letter asking if he could use Cotton as a reference for entrance into graduate school. The young man was an excellent student and Cotton had no problem with the request.

The other piece of mail was an envelope. He ripped it open and read a short message.

Stay out of it

It echoed the phone call that Cotton had received the previous week. He laid it down on his desk and stared at it. It's meaning was obvious – stay out of helping Mrs. Parker or any of the other minority members of the faculty. And who was the person who murdered Parker and attempted to harm the others? What connected these faculty or in Barton's case – the security force? Lavelle Hughes, Winston Scales, Greg Barton and Jesse Parker – what would their backgrounds show? Cunningham could request their files through Drew if it didn't get back to Regan. He would have to ask Drew whether it was still an active investigation even if it was handed over to the Buffalo Police. Still, he was getting messages. He was involved. And he didn't like being threatened. He would wait for the files and then proceed.

He had a leisurely meal with Jen as he discussed housing plans.

"What do you think of the house on Greenfield?" he asked.

"It's cute and it fits our needs," she said. "And I talked some more to the woman next door. Her name is Mrs. Davis. Did you know that she had a son who had Down Syndrome?"

"Had a son?"

"He died. The life expectancy for Down Syndrome kids is startling. It took her quite a while to get over it. I told her about Teddy, and she brightened up."

"When did you talk to her? Where was I?"

"Probably in the cellar talking to the real estate agent about a dry basement."

"I like it too. Kind of cozy. Out of the way, not much traffic."

"And the price is right," she said.

"I like the fireplace with the bookshelves on either side," he said.

They both looked at each other.

"Let's make another appointment to see it," she said.

And he agreed.

He was moving more and more of his things to Jen's apartment just so he could help her with the everyday cooking and cleaning. Occasionally, he would return home to retrieve some personal items or some books and papers pertinent to his work. On this evening, he went to collect his mail and pay his bills, but his thoughts never strayed far from the violence towards the minority members of campus and the possible student insurrection. Something was going to break soon.

Chapter 17

February 20

The meeting had been set for the 20th. Both Keegan and Kearns were in attendance as were members of YAWF (Youth Against War and Fascism) and a few other radical groups, both women and Black students. It was a cross section of student protest.

The meeting was set for Vice President Bennis' office. It was crowded and it soon was apparent that a larger conference room would have been a better venue. Most of the students knew each other except for the women's group and the Black organizations. Many women were dubious of the men, especially Black men who had been loath to take women seriously in the movement. It certainly didn't help when Stokely Carmichael, the leader of SNCC, the Student Non-Violent Coordinating Committee, said "The only position for women in the movement is prone."

"How are we supposed to come to any conclusions, if Regan isn't here?" asked a tousled hair lanky student whom he did not recognize.

Bennis was quick to answer.

"If anything comes up that needs the approval of the president, he is available, at short notice to come over to attend. As president, He has quite a few pressing issues to attend to, but he is aware of the serious nature of why we are here."

That did little to mollify the students, but they continued by stating their goals.

"Our goals are simple," said one of the leaders of SDS.

"Elimination of the college's cooperation with the government's war effort, the establishment of a free university and student participation in the hiring and firing of teachers. Those are some of the goals."

"Although, we are willing to discuss these things, quite a bit of discussion would need to take place. I'm sure that President Regan will agree to a student advisory committee on hiring, I don't think that allowing students to make the final decisions on such matters would be wise. On the other matters, I'm not quite sure what you mean by the College's cooperation with the government?"

"Project Themis for one," shouted out one of the students in the background.

"Project Themis is a rather benign program which has nothing to do with warfare."

"It's sponsored by the Department of Defense," said Keegan.

"The Department of Defense sponsors many projects that have nothing to do with making war," replied Bennis.

"So, you've relegated us to a passive observer in the hiring process and disregarded anything we say about a project sponsored by a department that is engaged in a unjust war in a foreign country. What else are you going to bullshit us with?" said Keegan.

At this point, the door opened, and President Regan stepped in. He maneuvered around the populace until he stood by Bennis. He was without a jacket, sleeves rolled up, glasses on a head with hair swept back. He struck a defiant pose.

"We have bent over backwards to continue with the same student – administration atmosphere that existed during President Meyerson's time here at the University. I was very disappointed over the ransacking of the ROTC offices last October. We could have made a much bigger deal about that situation and if we would have, some of you might not be here today."

There was a collective groan from the audience.

"I think meetings like this can be very constructive, but in the future any violence on this campus will not be tolerated. If I must bring in the sheriff I will do so."

One Black student from the back stepped forward.

"I believe that negotiations with the administration over stipends and hiring are going smoothly and I would hate to see that set back by violence on campus."

"That's good, that's good," said Regan. "Progress is being made."

"I believe our Black brothers are too optimistic about their situation," said Keegan.

"I ain't your brother," replied the Black man.

For a second the tension in the room dissipated like air being let out of a balloon. Then Kearns shot up and yelled.

"I'm not wasting my time anymore. It's plain that you don't give a shit about what we think is important. All we've heard here are threats. Well, something is coming down soon and it will shake this campus."

With that, he left the room, soon to be followed by other SDS members. The others stayed behind to see whether anything was going to be said. Regan shrugged his shoulders and left the room. Bennis lifted his hands, palms up to the group and they left.

Cotton looked over at Drew.

"That could have gone better."

"I never held any hope that it would. These people are miles apart. I expect something will happen in the next few days. I'm prepping my people on crowd control. I just don't know how many people we're talking about. It's not just UB students. There could even be high school students from Bennet or any other local schools. And then there's Canisius and Buffalo State. We might be talking about hundreds of kids.

They were both silent for a second. And then Cotton spoke. "I don't think there's a way to prepare ourselves. As they say in the Army, hope for the best, prepare for the worst."

COTTON and Jen went out to dinner that night, the first foray since the ill-fated *Your Host* visit. Fanny's restaurant in Amherst was a comfortable place and a step up from *Your Host*.

They found a comfortable window booth and settled in. Comfort was a priority with Jen's condition and Cotton was ever attentive. The words "how do you feel?" were beginning to get on Jen's nerves.

Cotton ordered a breakfast of eggs, pancakes, and sausage. Jen ordered a much milder dinner of a Caesar salad and apple sauce, although when the meals came, she eyed Cotton's with jealousy.

"Somethings been bothering you for a long time now and it's not worrying over my pregnancy," she said.

"I had a talk with Jefferson today after the meeting, which was an abject failure. We both agreed that a major confrontation is about to take place and that there's nothing we can do to prevent it."

"Can you talk with the students involved?" she asked.

"We tried everything. Neither side will listen to reason. The administration is being sanctimonious about the student's demands, even going to the point of letting them know if they incite violence, the Buffalo Sherriff's department will arrest them."

"Those assaults on the faculty members are on your mind also?"

"I've been warned off by Regan. He was very explicit."

"I guess will have to wait and see," she said adding house dressing to her salad.

Chapter 18

February 24

It began with an innocuous incident on the evening of the twenty-fourth. Black students were troubled by an inequity in stipends provided to Black basketball players. White radicals picked up the mantle of dissatisfaction and laid down on the basketball court in protest. And lo and behold, Erie County Sherriff's police cars were seen outside the gymnasium. The question uppermost in Cotton's mind was "Who called the cops?" He was aware of an Advisory Security Task Force that existed which comprised students, faculty and administration that was supposed to be involved in such a decision, but no one associated with that committee knew of any request. Besides, the time lapse between the courtside sit-down and the police arrival was slim. Perhaps an infiltrator had passed along the news, Cotton thought.

The next day, on the 25th, all hell broke loose. SDS scheduled a rally in Hass Lounge at Norton Union to boost their morale. After the meeting, which didn't produce the result their leaders intended, forty demonstrators took to the streets and proceeded to Hayes Hall. They were met by a cadre of security personal in full riot gear. Jefferson Drew stood with his men with Cotton off to the side.

President Regan stood on the steps and said to Drew, "Arrest these people!"

"We can't arrest that many people and so far, they haven't caused any violence or destruction of property."

Both Jefferson and Cotton knew that Drew's security force was not trained in such a situation. Hell, they thought, it would be a challenge for the Buffalo Police, who at that moment were arriving on campus.

By this time the students decided to retreat to Norton Hall with the security force marching in formation after them. Rocks were thrown and a general melee ensued. The students entered Norton and began to barricade themselves inside.

Drew instructed his security force to stand down in front of Norton Hall. At that moment, the sound of breaking glass echoed through the courtyard.

"There's your destruction of property," remarked Cotton.

"Better property than people's heads," said Drew.

As they approached Norton Union, they saw that a fight had developed between demonstrators and security police. In the middle of the struggle were Keegan and Kearns. Rocks were thrown, broken furniture legs were being used as clubs and Cotton and Drew threw themselves into the crowd. In the end Keegan and Kearns were dragged out of the struggle and thrown into a security car that had just arrived with lights flashing.

By this time, many of the students were leaving through side entrances. Cotton and Drew managed to disperse the rest of the demonstrators. They weren't interested in arresting as much as crowd control.

"The Sherriff's haven't left their cruisers yet," said Cotton.

"Yea, I talked to Amico. He said he was there for support. He was ready, if needed. He said it looked like the situation was well in hand. I think he was being a wise ass."

The scene was becoming more manageable now and security was ushering students away from the scene, Drew and Cotton proceeded into Norton Union to assess the damage.

It was mostly furniture. Chairs and tables were broken up to be used as clubs. Sofas were overturned in a defensive posture. Much of the furniture was used to barricade the doors as if the students were expecting an all-out security rush.

"Your men did OK," Cotton remarked while picking up the sharp-edged table leg.

"Oh, it could have been much worse, and the problem is I don't think it's over. I think that this is just the beginning. These demonstrators have got a taste of power and they're going to be back."

"I think you're right," said Cotton.

THE early morning of the next day, found Cotton, Drew and a few administrative people in President Regan's office.

"I assume those two students are in jail," said Regan.

"They'll post bail and be out by the afternoon," said Drew. "I checked downtown. They have plenty of people willing to post bail."

"They should be locked up with the key thrown away," said Regan. "I thought I made it clear that destruction of property would not be tolerated."

"In the heat of the moment, I don't think they were thinking rationally," said Cotton.

"What, are you on their side now?" said Bennis.

"I'm on the side of anyone who tries to keep things under control. Did you call Amico?" asked Cotton.

Everyone looked around but no one had the answer.

"I talked to Amico on site, and he said he didn't receive a call, but knew there was a problem and he wanted to be close by in case there was trouble." said Bennis.

"He got the information from the person infiltrating the SDS," said Drew.

"Regardless, we need to look at this situation and try to understand how we can prevent it from happening again," said Regan.

"I don't know if we can prevent it from happening, but we can try to engage in some sort of dialogue to prevent it from escalating. When they approached Hayes Hall, we could have tried to talk to their leaders. Once they got back to Norton, they were preparing for a siege," said Cotton.

Regan looked over at Drew. "What are your plans? How are you going to deploy your men?"

The military overtones of the request were not lost on the people in the room.

"Sir, my men are not trained to deal with crowd control, let alone arresting demonstrators. They hand out parking tickets, resolve roommate problems in the dorms, escort coeds to their cars at night, but they aren't used to getting hit by bricks."

"That's why we have the Buffalo Police as backup," said Regan. "Do we expect any more violence soon?"

Drew looked at Cotton who shrugged.

"I talked to a few students afterwards and they repeated the same thing. They said, this isn't over, and we'll be back.

A few said they were meeting later in the early morning. They mentioned the words "war council."

"I don't like the sound of that," said Regan. "Maybe we need to shut down the campus."

"Sir, I don't think that would work. We need to keep the appearances that everything is normal."

"Well, "said Regan, "Then what do we do?"

"Watchful waiting," said Cotton. "In the meantime, I'll try to get a hold of some of the people from SDS and see what I can do. If we can get by the next few days without any trouble, we should be good."

Chapter 19

February 25

Hugh Morrow was Governor Nelson Rockefeller's chief of staff, and he was passing on the governor's concerns about the violence on the UB campus over the phone to their recent hire.

"We can't have these incidents continue. The governor has expressed his displeasure over these events. We don't have murders on state campuses. I hope you have an idea about how to proceed."

"Not to worry. I'm firmly planted in Regan's office. I have the latitude in my position to move around campus with impunity. I'm meeting with staff and all the people involved in the minority incidents. Once I get a better grip on the situation, I'll get back to you."

He had flown to Buffalo, been introduced to Regan's staff, settled in an apartment, all in a matter of two weeks. He had contacted the police, read their reports, and even inserted himself into the scene in a very ingenious way.

"What can you do that the Buffalo Police can't?" asked Regan.

He smiled. "I have experience in these types of matters. I do my best work in an undercover situation."

He had a background with the Secret Service and the

FBI. He intended to use that experience to solve this problem. Another feather in his cap. He wasn't used to failure. But an unforeseen event caught him off his guard.

Chapter 20

February 26
9:15 PM

Cotton dropped off by Jefferson Drew's office the next day and found him pouring over an addition of *The Spectrum*, the student newspaper.

"Look at this," said Drew. Talk about stirring up the campus."

The headlines read "EXTRA!! INVASION."

"Well, in a sense, they're right," said Cotton.

"That's going to stir this campus up even more", said Drew. "As if that's possible."

"Read that section on the next page," invited Drew.

One of the campus police threw Kearns against the wall. A group of police began to club him until his head began to bleed. He was then handcuffed and dragged out as students, who we're leaving out the front door, pelted police with anything within reach.

"At least they mentioned the students pelting the police. It wasn't all one sided, "said Cotton.

"If that's an attempt at humor, it fell flat," said a grim-faced Drew.

"Now the primary concern must be to keep this from happening again," said Cotton.

"Cotton, we can't predict when and if this catastrophe will happen again. It could happen tonight for all we know."

"I could be mistaken," said Cotton, "but I think we've bought ourselves some time so we can work with some of the students, I don't think many of them were happy about what happened last night. Nothing positive came from it."

"There was one person who was satisfied with last night and that was Mike Amico. He must be smiling right now. He got his invitation into the campus."

Cotton left the building and strolled out into the early morning sunlight. Even the pleasant weather could not disguise the boarded-up windows and the broken furniture littering the area near Norton Hall.

His campus was crumbling. And in a few hours, it would come to a head.

Chapter 21

February 26
Early Afternoon

A security officer rushed into the room and yelled, "They're gathered in Norton Union in the lounge and they're talking about last night."

"How many?" asked Drew.

"Hundreds" he said.

"I better get over there," said Drew.

They both went and when they were within 50 yards of Norton, the crowd noise was apparent. As they approached the building a few students mulling around the entrance looked suspiciously at them. They entered a side door trying to be inconspicuous, but Drew in his official uniform stood out and Cotton's age and dress gave him away as administration.

They stood off to the side and listened to individual students account for the brutality they faced the evening before.

"I was standing there watching the protests when I was clubbed from behind," said one young woman who was holding the back of her head in mock indignation.

"We were attacked," said another student, a scruffy haired individual with a jean jacket and maroon bell bottoms. "We had no alternative but to defend ourselves."

The testimonials were interrupted by cries of "off the pigs" followed by shouts to march on Hayes Hall and, "get Regan." Which is what they did.

By this time, Drew had found a secluded place and used his walkie-talkie to notify all campus security to assemble at the front of campus near the Winspear entrance. The students, marching across the ROTC drill field, spied the security police in full riot gear and proceeded to march in tight formation. When they reached the edge of the field, they began to charge police, holding makeshift weapons that had acquired by ripping up ball field dugouts and other wooden structures. Along with stones and pieces of construction material they rained these weapons down on the security forces, The security units, that also contained members of the Buffalo Police department, were vastly outnumbered and moved off the campus down Winspear.

Cotton and Drew moved along the periphery of the rioters and watched in horror how the scene played out. Witnesses said later that there could have been a major incident if the number of Buffalo police had decided to defend the position with any weapons at their disposal.

Cotton and Drew were separated by the surging crowd which by this time was moving back towards the center of campus. Cotton noticed that there was a contingent of Erie County Sheriff Deputies headed by Mike Amico. Things were coming to a head and Cotton had no means to prevent it. He was relegated to the role of a helpless bystander. He was moving off to the side of one of the buildings to get out of the rush of the riot when he heard moaning. He located the source against the side of the building. A body had crumbled against the wall and was sliding down into the snow. Cotton rushed over and found the seemingly lifeless body of chemistry professor, Lavelle Hughes. It looked like he had been hit by a truck. His face was hardly recognizable. Cotton checked for a pulse and found a faint beat. He screamed over to a pair of co-eds to come and stay by the body while he searched for the nearest phone. He finally found a booth two blocks away. After he was assured that a ambulance was on its way, he raced back to where Hughes was and relieved the startled young women. He accompanied Hughes to Buffalo General Hospital where he was put into the intensive care unit listed in serious condition. Cotton sat in the waiting room at Buffalo General for a good part of the night. As he sat there, awaiting any report of Hughes condition, he had time to think. A multitude of questions came to him.

Why was Hughes, who before was terrified of harm, out that day, considering the potential danger from the rioting students? And more to the point, was this danger from stray bricks and debris thrown by students? Or was someone trying to kill him? Was the person who had messed with chemicals in his lab, trying again on a day where his assault might be attributed to someone else? From the looks of his wounds, it was hard to imagine he was the victim of a stray piece of brick or mortar. If that wasn't the case, it meant that the same person who killed Jesse Parker, almost ran over Greg Barton and mugged Winston Scales was still out there, roaming the campus, mixing with students and presenting a threat to minority faculty members. But, why?

Chapter 22

February 27

The next day roving groups of students roamed around campus entering buildings and causing disturbances. The general air around campus was one of tension and unease. Cotton went home early in the morning after receiving news that Hughes, while still in intensive care, was stabilized. He slept for a few hours until he received a call at 9:00 from Drew.

"We lost each other last night. Where did you end up?" asked Drew.

Cotton related his story about finding Lavelle Hughes. There was silence on the line for a few seconds until Drew spoke. "How is he?" he asked.

"Not in great shape, but they're hopeful that he will improve in the next twenty-four hours."

"Students were throwing all sorts of things – bricks rocks, pieces of wood from the ball field – It was not safe out there," Drew said.

"I'm not all that sure that he was hit by students. An occasional rock or piece of wood wouldn't have caused the damage that was inflicted on him," said Cotton.

"He could have been recognized by students as an academic and considered an enemy. You know, "off the pigs" doesn't always have to be cops," said Drew.

"I don't know," said Cotton. "Something doesn't seem right."

"Well, what are you going to do about it?" asked Drew.

"Nothing right now. I'm hoping that when Hughes regains consciousness, he 'll be able to tell us what happened."

Cotton would have loved to go back to bed, but although he didn't have a class till that evening, he felt due to all the disturbances on campus, he needed to be there, talk to student leaders, and try to calm things down.

After he showered, and shaved, he put on an outfit that consisted of a blue crew sweater, chinos and tan dessert boots. After he finished off a day-old calzone over the sink, he gave Jen a call to fill her in on all the details of the previous evening. Since she had become pregnant, Cotton was particularly sensitive to her being present at student uprisings. He had begun to escort her to her classes and drive her home after she was done.

"Tell me what happened yesterday," said Jen.

"There were too many students, and they pushed the police back to Winspear. After that it was a standoff between students and security and some of the Buffalo Police. It could have been disastrous. I saw one cop reach for his gun, but he was immediately calmed down. Amico with the Erie County Sheriff's Department was standing by waiting for an opening to enter campus."

"I know there is no love lost between you and that man," remarked Jen.

"He thinks that organized crime is not the main distributor of drugs in Buffalo. He's convinced that that the drug capital of our city is the university."

"That's ridiculous," said Jen. "I know the student body

well enough. Sure, there's pot and some hard drugs, but they're isolated instances. There is no drug king pin on campus."

"You're right, but Amico has it in for all students. He's worse than Regan."

"Not to change the subject, but Lavelle Hughes, why was he there?"

"I have no idea., but the funny thing is he's been very scared since the incidents in his lab with the chemicals being switched. I can't see him venturing out in what was possibly a dangerous situation."

"How bad was he hurt?" asked Jen.

"It wasn't a random brick or stone. He looked like he was involved in an automobile accident or as if he was mugged and beaten to a pulp. He's lucky if he survives without brain damage."

"I wonder what *The Spectrum* is going to say about it?" she asked. The Spectrum was the student newspaper.

"The Spectrum is going to call it a police riot where officers got out of control and brutalized students. They will probably say that Lavelle Hughes was attacked by authorities and beaten senseless."

She agreed that Cotton would pick her up outside her apartment in twenty minutes She was there waiting, wrapped in a heavy winter coat with a parka pulled up over her head. She had pressed blue jeans, and fur lined boots. She moved slowly into the passenger seat, gave Cotton a peck on the cheek and they resumed their conversation.

"What are your plans for the day?" she asked.

"Well, I don't have a class until tonight. I'm going to get some paperwork done, you know, correct papers, plan for courses. I might wander around the Union, see if I can talk to some of the radicals and get them calmed down. What about you?"

"Same as you, course work with a committee meeting thrown in there."

"When do you plan on being done?" asked Cotton.

"Around four," she said.

"I'll come and get you and drive you back to your place."

"I have a pregnancy urge for a Santora's pizza," she said.

"You don't have to be pregnant to want that," he laughed. "See you at four."

In his office there were a mound of papers to correct and plenty of planning, especially for his evening class on the Gilded Age. It was one of his favorite classes. The students were alive and full of questions. And there were a few radicals in there that he could talk to after class to see what was brewing.

Mid way through the afternoon, Greg Barton appeared in his doorway.

"Got a minute?" he asked.

"Sure, let me clear a chair." said Cotton. "What's up?"

Barton was uneasy when he settled himself in the chair.

"Morale is down in security. Jefferson Drew is on edge. I've never seen him like this. I figured you might have an idea about where this is going. You know, what students are saying."

Cotton pushed aside the papers he had been correcting, knitted his hands and heaved a sigh.

"The students are very upset. They don't think that they have a voice in what's happening on campus. They believe that Regan is just threatening and not listening."

"A lot of the security people are not trained for large

scale crowd control. I've served with the Cleveland Police department, and I think I've got a handle on what to do in riot conditions. The fact is we are outnumbered in a lot of these situations. That means we must rely on the Buffalo Police for backup. And the Erie County Sherriff's Department is just waiting to patrol this campus. We can't have three different law enforcement agencies vying for control."

"I agree with everything that you've said," said Cotton. The only thing I can try to do is talk to the various organizations and their leaders and to see if I can get them to see reason on some of these issues."

"Well, you better act fast because something violent is going to happen and news crews are going to be coming to Buffalo. I saw a Buffalo cop pulling his gun the other day. He was shouted down by the officer in charge, but he was that close to firing. And what about Lavelle Hughes? How did he get beat up so bad? Was that from the demonstrators?"

Cunningham looked grim. "I heard about the pulled gun. And I don't know about Hughes. I spent some time with him at the hospital and I think he'll pull through. I plan to go out today and see who I can find. Tell me about your experience with the Cleveland Police force."

"Jefferson Drew convinced me to take this job. He said that it would be a step towards a job with the Buffalo Police Department. My father was Police Chief in Cleveland and I wanted to get out from under his wing. Didn't want people to think I got a job because of him."

Barton was not satisfied when he left Cunningham's office. Neither was Cunningham. When he finished correcting and planning the evening's class, he went out to search the campus for anyone who might be the answer.

The winter meant darkness would creep on the day sooner. Cotton called Jen and confirmed their pick-up time. He drifted into Norton Hall just as people were looking for something for dinner. He was in luck as he just saw Kearns get in line for food. Cotton slipped in behind him.

"Buy you dinner?" he asked.

Kearns looked back suspiciously.

"Accepting a meal from the wrong side might look bad. But I'll risk it."

They proceeded through the food line. Kearns picking out the meal of the day – meat loaf with mashed potatoes and gravy and Cunningham, thinking of the pizza waiting for him later, went with a salad. They took a seat far away in the corner.

"OK, Professor Cunningham, what's on your mind?"

Cotton smiled. "It's not what's on my mind, it's what's on yours. What's planned for the next few days?

Kearns looked annoyed. "I don't particularly like being pumped for information."

"Look, neither one of us wants a repeat of what happened the other day. Somebody is going to seriously hurt. I just want saner heads to get together and talk."

"And what happened the last time we got together? Pig Regan made threats and denied us an opportunity to participate in decision making."

"I know how that went down. I will try to talk with Regan in the next few days about being more compromising in his approach. I just want a promise that in the meantime, that you and others will try to postpone any demonstrations."

"Listen professor, I can't control what the masses do. You work under the misconception that a few people have absolute control over thousands of individuals. We give speeches, we listen to people tell their stories and after we disband, the group goes where they will. We're also affected by what we hear in the news. If some event like an uptick in bombing or a horrendous event such as My Lai takes place, we might feel like we want the college to take notice."

Cotton nodded. "What you want the college to do is recognize these events and announce that they understand the effect it has on people."

"Of course!" said Kearns. "Why wouldn't they? We want a college that isn't an institution apart from society. I understand that its main purpose is to educate people, but it also should be responsive to the needs of society. It can't just ignore what is going on in the world."

Cotton was impressed with the sincerity of Kearns' words.

"I will take your message to the president and get back to you. Do I have a promise that you will work towards de-escalating the violence on campus?"

"I can't promise, but I will do nothing as an individual to cause violence."

Cotton left the meeting with a small vestige of hope that some progress had been made. He called Regan when he returned to his office and a meeting was set up for the following day. Then he went to pick up Jen. They travelled to Santora's and picked up their meals. They made they way up to Jen's apartment, cleared the kitchen table and sat.

"It sounds like Kearns is a decent human being," said Jen, munching on a slice of pizza.

"He had some valid points, I'll admit," said Cotton "I have a meeting set up tomorrow with Regan"

"From what you've told me, Regan views certain issues as non-negotiable," she said.

"He was particularly upset over the violence at the ROTC offices last October. He reacts very strongly to student violence of any kind. And he also believes that most of the student body that just wants an education, should not be intimidated by a minority of violent students."

"Is he responsive to the demands of the protesters?" she asked.

"He views many of the demands to be outrageous, Like College A and demands to fire certain coaches. I even admit that College A is way too lax in their demands on students and their grading. And coaches like Surfestini will never be fired. He's on the verge of retirement anyways."

"I hope something will come out of your meeting. Maybe you should have some backup, like Drew."

"I hear that he stressed out enough. He doesn't have the manpower to handle these rioters. He must rely on the Buffalo Police. They've been on the campus on and off for days."

"I believe that Regan's on the edge and he won't tolerate much more from the activists. We'll see tomorrow."

Chapter 23

February 28

Cotton was right on time for his meeting with Regan. Regan's secretary said he was on the phone and would meet with him shortly. The waiting room was spacious with paintings on the walls, mostly Audubon prints neatly framed and matted. The furniture was chrome, unlike Meyerson's décor which was usually heavy oak. Cotton fiddled with some fund-raising brochures until the secretary received a phone call.

"You can go on in. He's ready to receive you," she said.

Cotton entered the room, and his first impression of Regan's appearance was that the man had aged since their last meeting. Fundraising, ordinary administrative duties and faculty problems are usually stressful enough for a University President. Now Regan had to deal with a university that was teetering on the verge of anarchy. Deep circles under his eyes and a perpetual look of disgust clouded his features.

"How are you, sir?" asked Cotton, already knowing the answer.

Regan let out a low laugh.

"That was Albany, and the governor wants to know how things are going on one of his flagship universities. I almost told him we were doing what we could to keep the boat afloat. Instead, I told him we were experiencing problems like most large urban universities, but we were determined to make sure that each student would receive a quality education and with that in mind, I would do whatever necessary to achieve that goal.

"Yes, sir," said Cotton.

"And having said that Cunningham, what can you relate to me about the current climate among our radical population?"

"I don't think I can tell you anything new. Across campus, there are smaller demonstrations, students marching, chanting slogans and such. But there is very little destruction of property and certainly no disruption of classes."

"Well, that's a relief, but do you think that this is just the calm before another storm?"

"I'm concerned about that, sir. None of their requests have been answered and any event on the national scene could set off their rancor."

"None of their requests will be answered, I assure you. I will not turn the reins of this University over to a bunch of hoodlums. Their demands are ludicrous. College A is a joke. Marty went too far in allowing that. Imagine students grading their own papers? Deciding whether they pass or fail?"

"Meyerson was trying to give the students some ownership in the education process. Perhaps it went out of control."

Regan grimaced and then smiled.

"You always were one of Myerson's chosen few, weren't you, Cunningham? Well, he's now longer here and I must carry on. He left before things heated up. I guess I can't blame him. He had other opportunities and I hear that the Ivy League is calling him."

"Yes, I hear the University of Pennsylvania," said Cotton.

Regan swiveled his chair and looked out his window. It gave him a wide panoramic view of campus. It was a dull lifeless day, with snowbanks darkened by the stain of grass on mud. Buffalo was not a picturesque university such as Vanderbilt, nor had it the centuries old tradition of a Harvard or Yale. It was a gritty urban campus, highly ranked, yet bereft of an attractive educational tradition.

"It's a lonely job, Cotton," he said, in a rare moment of informality. "No matter what happens, I will be held accountable. My reputation will rise, or fall based on the decisions that I make."

"Don't be too hard on yourself, sir. Some things are beyond our control."

"Not out of our control, Cunningham, not out of our control. And I will meet force with force if necessary."

He had a determined look on his face when Cotton left his office.

As Cotton walked across campus, a light rain was falling. He pulled up the hood of his jacket over his head and thought of what could possibly come. He had no control over what the radicals would do. They would talk to him, but they wouldn't listen to him.

He entered Diefendorf Hall, and trudged up the stairs to the department office and checked his mail.

"You have a visitor" said the secretary with a smile, "I didn't think you would mind if I unlocked your office and let him in."

Puzzled, he continued to his office and to his utter surprise, seated in a visitor's chair was Martin Meyerson, the former UB President.

"Sir, what a pleasant surprise. I didn't know you were on campus."

"I didn't let anybody know. I wanted to talk with some old friends, you included," Meyerson said.

"I'm glad you consider me in that regard, sir," said Cotton.

Meyerson resumed his seat and crossed his legs. He was wearing a subdued brown pinstripe suit with a blue button-down shirt and a beige tie. His neatly folded trench coat lay on a seat beside him.

"Cotton, I know what you've been going through since I left. I feel a sense of guilt for leaving UB in such a precarious position, but the lot of a university president can be a short one and you must grab at positions if they're open. The University of Pennsylvania is a prestigious Ivy League job and I also have connections to the city, both professional and family. It was a logical choice."

"I understand, sir," said Cotton.

"How is Regan doing?" asked Meyerson.

"Well, I don't have the connection that I did with you. He made it clear that I wasn't to involve myself in any police situation."

"Have there been any?" asked Meyerson.

Cotton proceeded to explain to Meyerson the situation with the death of Jesse Parker and the assaults on the others. Meyerson's face took on a grim tone.

"That's no good, Cunningham, no good at all. It's a mark on the University system. Have you made any progress?"

Cunningham took note of the irony in Meyerson's statement.

"I 've been asked to look into it by Parker's wife and also by the chemistry professor, who by the way was seriously injured during a student demonstration."

Meyerson was stunned.

"People are being seriously injured. How could things have gotten this bad?"

"I don't believe he was injured by part of the demonstration. I think whoever is behind this campaign against minority faculty singled him out."

"Maybe this is a police matter," Meyerson said.

'The police have investigated and come up with nothing to indicate a pattern. They believe they are random acts."

"What do you think, Cunningham?"

"I believe they're connected and will keep occurring until someone else is killed."

Meyerson switched topics.

"Regan is old school and was in the army in both WWII and Korea. He believes in rank, and he also thinks that orders should be followed regardless of their impact. I wondered how he would work out."

"I believe he has good intentions but a short fuse. He doesn't believe in compromise."

Meyerson picked up his hat and coat.

"I wish you well, Cunningham. I believe the future of this campus is directly tied into what happens across a broad swath of our society. The war, civil rights, the draft – they all affect the campus climate. College isn't' just about choosing courses and doing well in school. Students want a voice, and they want the university to reflect their mores."

He left as unceremoniously as he came.

Cotton sat down in his office chair and thought about Meyerson's visit. If Meyerson was right, there was more conflict to come and with murder right in the middle.

Chapter 24

March 3

Cotton was studying last week's edition of *The Spectrum*. Franky Valli and the Four Seasons were in town, Joe Frasier had just taken out Jimmy Ellis in a heavyweight match, the Doghouse was offering 89 cents specials, and Jane Fonda was staring in a new movie called, "They Shoot Horses, Don't They?"

The biggest news was on the front page. The Chicago 7 plus Bobby Seale had just been sentenced to 20 years in contempt charges. The paper was broken up into students' responses in various cities. In most places from Seattle and Berkely to Columbia, students were rioting in the streets. Thousands of protesters were making war against the establishment in what they thought was a miscarriage of justice.

The Chicago Seven was made up of a disparate group of individuals, all who had been at the Democratic National Convention in 1968 and were charged with conspiracy and crossing state lines to incite a riot. Rennie Davis, David Dellinger, John Froines, Tom Hayden, Abbie Hoffman, Jerry Rubin and Lee Weiner were the defendants.

Other issues were coming up on campus. Students were accusing Regan of massive incompliance. There were talks of student strikes and actions against the university. There was a constant Buffalo Police presence on campus.

Cotton and Jen were moving ahead on the place in Wanakah. They decided to see it again to solidify that decision and they were taking Teddy with them.

As usual, Teddy was happy to see them and bounced back and forth in the back seat, uttering single words as they drove down Route Five to the house. When they pulled into the driveway, he hopped out and scurried about in both the Greenfield address and the land next door. Soon, the door opened and the woman that Jen had talked to previously strolled out.

"Well, hello," she said to a startled Teddy who had pulled up right in front of her.

"I'm sorry, Mrs. Davis. Teddy didn't mean to be a problem."

"That's perfectly all right, my dear. You go ahead and look at the house and I'll take Teddy inside for some milk and cookies."

Jen and Cotton were astonished when the short haired blond woman took Teddy's hand and brought him right along. Teddy looked over his shoulder for affirmation from Cotton and when he smiled, he went in with her.

"Can you believe what we just saw?" asked Jen.

"No, I can't believe it. She seemed perfectly at home with Teddy."

"I think I know why, "said Jen. "When we spoke a few weeks ago she mentioned that Billy, died six months ago. She said she's been lost ever since."

When they were done looking over the house and property, they were now sure that this was the place they needed and having a neighbor, sympathetic to the needs of a Down's child was another plus.

Chapter 25

March 4

Cotton was sitting in Jefferson Drew's office and listening to Drew complain about the mounting problems on campus.

"Can you believe it; the students have called upon Regan to appear before a people's court. Besides the charge of him being a "war criminal" they're also accusing him of incompetency. Now I don't know about the incompetency, but the war criminal charge is outrageous. Some of these students, Cotton, are pampered, upper class snips with no sense of reality."

Cotton was leaning back in a director's chair. As usual, the temperature was slightly over sixty. Cotton never took off his winter jacket while in Drew's office. He didn't know whether the heating system wasn't up to task or that Drew enjoyed the spartan existence.

"I do believe that sometimes their sense of reality suffers. They tie Reagan into what's happening on the national and international scene. They're challenging the college to take a stand on issues that the college isn't prepared to do. Do you have any news about what the student radicals are planning?"

"We're running around putting out brush fires. By "we",

I mean our security police and the Buffalo Police who have pretty much taken up residence on campus. Don't get me wrong, they've been helpful. Our security police are useless against student crowds between 500 and 1000 students."

"Marty Meyerson showed up, out of the blue at my office the other day."

Drew hitched up in his chair, a look of surprise on his face.

"What did he have to say?" asked Drew.

"Not much. He was concerned about the level of violence on campus. He didn't say a word against Regan. He was part of the process that picked him. Talking to him, reminded me of the tight relationship we had with him when he was president. That's something that's missing these days."

"I know what you mean, the three of us worked well together," said Drew.

"Somehow," Cotton said, "we have to get through this with a President that has a short fuse and doesn't care much for the radical fringe of students."

"I call it the lunatic fringe," said Drew.

COTTON visited Lavelle Hughes at Buffalo General Hospital later that day and he was surprised to see a police presence outside his door. Cotton knew the officer on guard. Jimmy Hines was just joining the force when Cotton was exiting it.

"Hey, Jimmy, what's up? Have there been problems with Hughes?"

"Hey, Cotton. Yea, there have been. A few days after Hughes got this room, there was an incident with a visitor. It happened late at night. Hughes woke up and swears he saw a man next to his bed fooling around with the IV. He knew it wasn't an orderly or doctor, so he screamed, and the man disappeared. The next day, Hughes called the Buffalo Police and pleaded for an armed guard outside his room. He said he had experienced threats while teaching at UB and was sure someone was out to get him."

"He's right, Jimmy. The Buffalo Police have a record of attempted harm on minority faculty on campus, The police probably took it to heart when they stationed you here."

When Cotton entered the room, he found Hughes sleeping. After a few minutes standing by his bedside, Hughes opened his eyes.

"I am glad to see someone from the college. I was beginning to think that they had forgotten that I work there."

"Lavelle, I'm sorry about what happened to you. First, I've come to see how you're doing and then I want to shed some light on why this all happened,"

"Well look at me. I'm all bruised and battered. And on pain pills all the time. And the pills don't work half the time. I'm a wreck."

And he looked it. Cotton found it hard to look upon a face with that much damage.

"I'm sorry to hear that you've suffered so. I need to ask you some questions, if you're up to it."

"If it's going to lead to solving this situation, I'll do anything."

"First of all, what were you doing out in all the turmoil that day? I would think you would want to avoid all that."

"You're right. It was a terrible decision on my part. I was visiting a friend on that part of the campus and when we heard all the noise, we were curious. My friend wouldn't step outside, but since most of the demonstrations had moved past us, I thought it was safe. I walked out into his back yard and stood for a while. Suddenly I was grabbed from behind, wrestled to the ground and beaten. Later, the police found a rock with blood on it that my assailant had used. Don't ask me for a description because after the first few blows, I passed out. I woke up a day later in intensive care. Believe me, Cotton, I'm scared shitless. To be attacked in the hospital, a place you believe is safe, well I can't sleep wondering whether my life is still in danger."

"I think you're all right now, Lavelle. You've got an armed guard outside, and I'll check on you every day, either in person or on the phone. If there's anything that you need from home, just call me."

Lavelle said he had friends bringing in what he needed but thanked Cotton for his concern. Cotton left, still in the dark about what was causing all this.

Chapter 26

March 13

When Cotton got to his office door the next day, he found a bedraggled young student leaning against his door. Without asking any questions, he opened his door, swept off a chair and motioned him to sit.

"How can I help? I don't think I have you in any of my classes," said Cotton.

"I'm not here as a student, professor. I'm here as a paid informant of the Buffalo Police Department. I won't mention my name and I hope you'll forget me after I leave today, but I have some information and I didn't know how to continue."

Cotton motioned for his to proceed.

"I'm sure you remember the uprising a few weeks ago and the assault on the college professor."

"Yes, I do. I've been visiting him in the hospital, and he is currently under police protection."

The informant sat back in the chair.

"I wasn't aware of that. It makes the information I'm giving you even more important."

"What information?" asked Cotton impatiently.

"There was security footage taken of the whole event. Don't ask me by whom but at one point in the event the camera veered off into another direction and picked up some footage of Professor Hughes."

"And?" said Cotton.

"What it showed was very disturbing."

"What did it show?"

"It shows an assault on the professor, which is disturbing enough, but it also gives a clue as to who the assailant might be."

Cotton waited for the shoe to fall.

"Although the footage is grainy, it shows that the assailant had a security uniform on."

"What security?"

"Campus security. Jefferson Drew's men."

"Was there any positive facial recognition?"

"None, only that it was one of his men. And I'm coming to you because of your position at the college. You're close to Drew, but I think you're still impartial enough to handle this information. If I go to Drew, how can I be assured of his impartiality?"

"I see your predicament. I'm as anxious as anyone to make sure Hughes is safe. I promised him I would investigate the matter of the minority faculty's safety. This adds another layer to the problem. And it's a touchy matter to include Jefferson Drew's men."

The informant rose and moved towards the door. Before he did, he left a packet on Cotton's desk.

"I would appreciate you forgetting we ever had this meeting,"

He exited just as he had appeared on the scene.

Cotton muddled over the problem. How could he approach Drew with this information? If it was one of his men, it would be a terrible indictment of his chain of command. He wondered, at first if he should take it up with Regan. He decided in the end that he owed a certain allegiance to Drew and that he would meet with him to discuss the matter.

The meeting took place later in the day and it wasn't a pleasant one.

After Cotton explained what the informant said, Drew exploded.

"Who is this informant and where is he getting his information?"

"Jefferson, he never gave his name or revealed where he got his information."

"Then for all we know, his accusations could be bogus. He might be part of some plot to discredit our security force."

"That could be, but how do you explain these pictures?"

He opened the packet that the informant had left and put three pictures on Drew's desk.

Drew took quite a while examining the pictures and when he was done, he sat back with a discouraged look on his face.

"What do you see in these pics?" he asked.

"The images are grainy, but I see someone with a security uniform kicking the shit out of a helpless victim."

"I see that also, but could it have been one of my officers getting a bit overzealous with a violent protester?"

"Jefferson, this wasn't in the middle of a protest demonstration, it was way off to the side, in an area that corresponds to where Hughes was. And the victim seems Black."

"Cotton, I agree with you. These pictures are damning evidence against my bureau. I need to do some investigating on my own. I only ask you to not share this information with anyone else."

"Jefferson, if this evidence truly indicts someone on your force, then at some time, that information will have to go further than both of us. Right now, I'm probably in trouble for not taking this evidence to Regan as soon as I got it."

"Cotton, just give me some time to clean my house. This is a terrible mark on my department and my command. I promise that I won't keep this information private for very long."

Cotton left Drew's office with a bad taste in his mouth. He knew what he just agreed to was wrong, but he had a relationship with Drew going back to when they solved cases together. He wasn't about to abandon that. He had decided to give Drew the time. But the question uppermost in his mind was an obvious one. Who was in those pictures?

Chapter 27

March 15

The news was out that fifty faculty had been arrested due to their participation in a Hayes Hall sit-in to protest police presence on campus. They had begun their sit-in at 1:00 PM and by 2:00, they were being ushered into K-9 wagons in the back of the building. They were booked at police headquarters and released on their own recognizance. They were to return the next day to post bail which was originally $100 but had since been raised to $500. The courts were not inclined towards leniency.

Cotton was having coffee with one of the defendants in Norton Hall. George Devine had been friends with Cotton since their graduate days.

"Cotton, we just felt that we had to make a statement. Through all the student protests we were relatively quiet, but as teachers, we needed to show the students that what we had preached should be supported by us outside the confines of the classroom."

"I hear Judge Mattias has it out for you guys."

"Yes, and he's upped bail from the original $100 to $500. That's a lot of money for some of us who are adjunct. We are really going to feel the pinch."

"I heard that some of you are on some sort of peace patrol?"

"I'm not involved but some of my friends are. It's not an easy job. Sometimes you must stand between students who are throwing rocks and police who like to swing batons."

They finished their coffee and Cotton proceeded back to his office in Diefendorf Hall. On his way back through the mist that had fallen on the campus, his thoughts moved from campus affairs to things more domestic.

Things had proceeded quickly on the house. Their bid was accepted, and they were granted early entry. So, the next day found Cotton, Jen and Teddy driving over to the house to see what needed to be done before they could move in.

When they pulled into the driveway, Mrs. Davis popped out of her house in greeting.

"I would be glad to watch Teddy while you two get some work done on the house. I've got some games I used to play with my own child and there's always cookies and milk."

"Mrs. Davis, I wouldn't want to inconvenience you," said Jen.

"My dear, you don't understand. In my life the only inconvenience is loneliness. Teddy can help me as much as I can help him."

Teddy seemed to be very eager to spend time with Mrs. Davis. It did make things easier when they came to work on the house. Although Jen being a few months pregnant, meant a few breaks in the action.

The house was a small two-story Cape Cod with two small bedrooms upstairs. The downstairs featured a formal living room with a tiny bedroom off to the side. A combined dining room kitchen and a single bathroom completed the affair. The door off the kitchen led to a single car garage. It would be a treat to not have to scrape the snow of the car in the winter, thought Cotton. Everything was small, but it was all comfortable.

Cotton and Jen made some preliminary measurements for curtains, debated over which rooms needed a fresh coat of paint and calculated on how their furniture would fit into various rooms.

When they took a break, they sat down on a few chairs that had been left behind and discussed Teddy's predicament.

"Jen, a few ideas have popped into my head since we've developed a relationship with Mrs. Davis."

"Yes?" asked Jen.

"We both know how sad Teddy has been at the group home. I mean, every time he sees us, he jumps for joy."

"Yes?"

"Well, I just think that Teddy could spend a lot more time with us once we move in, especially with Mrs. Davis' help."

"Cotton let's not jump too much ahead of ourselves. I'm sure what you say is true, but let's see how they develop. And you must speak with your sister about all this."

Whet they knocked on Mrs. Davis' door and received permission to enter, they were greeted by Teddy who had frosting all over his mouth and a big grin on his face

"We were frosting cookies," said Mrs. Davis with a smile. Please come in and help me eat them. It's too many calories for an old woman to have around."

So they all ended up sitting at a kitchen counter, munching on cutout cookies and drinking milk.

"When my boy was young, I did cutout cookies as a way for him to understand different shapes and objects.

He had to say them before he ate them. It's a great incentive."

Jen was looking up at a framed picture on a kitchen shelf.

Mrs. Davis caught her glance.

"That was my Billy. He lived until he was twenty-five. I had that long with him and I'm thankful for it. Downs kids don't live very long lives."

Teddy was looking at the picture and the concentration was unlike him. He seemed fascinated by the picture, almost like he was seeing something of himself in it.

When it came time to leave, Teddy resisted. It was usual for him to not want to go back to the group home, but it was usually because he didn't want to leave Cotton. Now Cotton sensed it was different. He didn't want to leave Mrs. Davis' house.

"I want you to know that that you all are welcome in this house, especially this young man," she said putting an arm around his shoulders. Strangely enough, in response to this gesture of affection, he leaned his head and rested it on her.

As they left the house, Jen and Cotton were speechless. Teddy was never one to show great instances of emotion. Although he smiled all the time, he generally shied away from touch. When he had his earphones on, listening to music, Cotton and Jen were free to speak.

"What did you think of that?" asked Jen.

"I have been with Teddy for his whole life and I have never seen him react like that. For him to show affection to someone he's known for a few weeks, is unbelievable. I know that he hates where he lives, but still…."

"Talk to your sister, Cotton."

Cotton knew exactly what she was talking about.

Chapter 28

The Middle of April

The days passed with minor police skirmishes and occasional student strikes which kept them away from the classroom. Savoy Brown was appearing as part of a blues festival, Pizza Hut was offering fantastic deals on pizza. and The Buffalo Braves, the cities' new entry in the National Basketball Association, was hiring Dolph Shayes to coach the team. Lavelle Hughes was out of the hospital and resuming his teaching duties and Cotton and Jen were relieved to be going back to the simple duties of teaching. They had moved into their new house and were using their spare time with minor details in decoration. They were even enjoying driving in together in the morning.

Working in his office that morning, a figure appeared in his doorway. Jefferson Drew asked, "May I come in?"

"Sure, come on in and find a seat."

Drew, shut the door after he entered and sat on a chair in front of the bookshelves. He was nervous.

"I hate to even mention this, because it implicates one of my men, but I think I've found out who the security officer in that footage is," said Drew.

"I'm listening," said Cotton.

"I think it was Greg Barton," said Drew.

Cotton was taken aback.

"Why Barton?" asked Cotton.

Drew hesitated. "Because I can recognize his gait, the way he moves. He's like an athlete."

Cotton had viewed the same pictures, but he had not reached the same conclusions.

"Do you have any other evidence?" asked Cotton.

"I know where my men were at that moment. Most of them were on the road where the bulk of protesters were. I checked with all my force. Everyone was within view, accounted for except for Barton."

"So," said Cotton. "What do you do now?'

"Well, I thought that you gave me a certain amount of time before it had to be reported to the administration. I'm ready to move on that and initiate an investigation into Greg Barton."

Cotton was confused. He always viewed Barton as an exceptional police officer who played it strictly by the book. Being a Black man, why would he be assaulting Lavelle Hughes? In fact, this information would make him a prime suspect on all the attacks on minority candidates, including the death of Jesse Parker. What was his motive?

"I appreciate you coming to me with this information," said Cotton. "I'll deliver it to the authorities."

"Look, Cotton, I feel terrible about this. I hire these people. I thought Greg was one of the most outstanding candidates I'd ever met. But he was always tightly wired. I think something just snapped."

Drew left Cotton's office with his head down. He was very despondent over the whole matter.

Later in the afternoon, there was a knock on his door and Greg Barton appeared. After Cotton welcomed him in, he settled, hat in hand, into one of Cotton's chairs.

"I didn't exactly know who to go to on this matter. I hope I can count on your confidentiality."

"As long as it not something that I deem appropriate to relate to the authorities. But go ahead, I'll let you know if problems come up."

Barton was in obvious discomfort when he related his story.

"I have this feeling that I'm being watched by my own people. My fellow security officers are treating me different and even Drew is acting strange. It has to do with the recent demonstration on campus and what happened to Lavelle Hughes. I was questioned about my whereabouts during that demonstration."

Cotton listened to the whole story and had to think quickly. What should he reveal to Barton about Drew's accusations? He decided to play it conservatively.

"Lavelle Hughes beating is a serious incident. Security footage indicates that a member of your group might be implicated. An investigation is being held. All the members are being questioned. That's all I know."

Barton left Cotton's office with a dissatisfied look on his face. He felt he was being accused of something and he didn't like it.

Cotton decided that he wasn't going to say anything to Regan right away. There were too many questions to be answered, too much information to be followed up on. He needed time to sort things out. He hoped he wouldn't have to wait too long. The killer might become impatient.

Chapter 29

The Beginning of May

With the mid spring warm weather descending on campus, the outdoor demonstrations and marches began to multiply. The tension in the air amped up as circumstances on the national scene regarding the war became complicated. News of President Nixon extending the war into Cambodia in the form of a bombing campaign became public. The nation felt duped by the government. Trust in the administration was wavering, especially among young people.

This dissatisfaction was apparent to Cotton in his classes.

"I can't keep my mind on my studies with all the things going on across the country," said Ned Fletcher, a senior from Orchard Park, New York. "There's talk of a student strike. I might not be able to finish the year. I need to graduate. I have a job waiting for me when I leave college."

Judy Young, a junior from Nashville, did not sympathize. "What's happening in the world affects millions of people, here and abroad. Your little world pales by comparison. We can't just think of ourselves."

Voices rose as students in the room began to take sides. Cotton did not object. He decided it was a teaching moment. Besides, they needed to let off some steam.

As he left the room, a group of students walked out with him. Sometimes hallway conversations were valuable.

"Where do you stand, Professor?" asked more than one student.

"I feel the tension and I sympathize with you. When I was a student, things weren't as complicated. It was the mid-fifties, and protests were not part of the scene. We were a contented nation, fresh out of two wars and all we wanted was normalcy. That wasn't going to last very long, and then the sixties exploded."

That didn't satisfy the students. The fifties were a foreign land occupied by their parents who lived far away from their ideals.

COTTON was in his sister's kitchen discussing Teddy's situation while she was fixing supper for her family.

"I'm glad you're happy," said Cotton.

"There's a lot less stress now that Teddy's where he should be," she said.

Cotton still believed she was in denial, but his accusations of that months before had led to a split in the family.

"I want to talk to you about Teddy," he said.

She stiffened. "What about Teddy?" she asked suspiciously.

"I still think that the group home is not the answer. He's not happy there. The only time he seems content is when he comes home for a visit or comes with me."

"Cotton, I don't see where you're going with this?"

"I want him to come and live with Jen and me on a trial basis."

His sister was speechless. When she recovered, she spat out her answer.

"Why would you do that?"

"Because I think he could fit in with us. I checked the local school system. They have special provisions for such a child."

"What about when he gets off the bus or when you both are gone?"

"There is a woman next door who has agreed to provide care for him when we're not there. She has previous experience with a Downs child and she's more than glad to help."

After a moment's pause, she said, "I must talk this over with my husband. Teddy's his child too."

Cotton had to laugh to himself. Her husband was the one who had issued a previous ultimatum. Teddy goes or I leave.

They left it at that.

Chapter 30

Kent State and After

On May 4, 1970, the seminal event of the tumultuous Vietnam era took place. Kent State will forever be remembered for a picture of student Allison Krause bending over a body of a fellow student. The shootings occurred when the National Guard, riled up by students throwing rocks in their direction, opened fire. Her face mirrored the anguish of a generation. This event and the escalated war effort featuring the bombing in Cambodia, triggered a national response.

Cotton knew that the university he taught at was not immune to such a display of violence. Colleges across the country were enveloped in crisis. Students across the nation were participants in uprisings that were challenging the central premise of higher learning. And they weren't doing it through peaceful debate. They were doing it through revolution.

His worst fears came true when on May 8th, UB demonstrators followed the path of the fellow students across the country in an uprising that precipitated the firing of buckshot into the crowd of students.

In the early afternoon, roving crowds of students congregating around Norton Union started the affair. Soon a contingent of security officers, Buffalo Police and Erie County Deputies were called in to quell the proceedings. According to the police, the demonstrators attacked with rocks, and bricks. According to the students, the police instigated by firing buckshot into the crowd which caused several students to be taken in for emergency medical care. They then tear gassed the crowd which ultimately enveloped the area and caused more causalities. The police of course denied the buckshot rumor but could hardly get away with denying the gas that permeated half of the campus.

Cotton Cunningham found himself in the thick of this for various reasons. He was just crossing campus when it happened, and he also realized that several of his students were suffering from the various aftereffects of the gas and buckshot. One of the students, Janice Daily from Cotton's afternoon class, staggered over and sought his aid.

He immediately led her and a few other companions to a first aid station in an adjacent building. After depositing them there and being assured of their safety, he went out to make himself helpful in some way.

He was a witness to more buckshot fired, but the tear gas that was expended presented a particular problem. It disoriented students and made them act like zombies stumbling along in some movie in an apocalyptic setting.

He made his way through the gas with a handkerchief over his face and tears streaming down his face. The authorities were all protected by gas masks, and it was hard to discern what was happening. Before he exited the scene for his own safety, he believed he saw a man in a security uniform dragging a limp body over to the side of a nearby building, Curious about this incident, he followed at a distance and saw the figure load the body into a car and slowly pull away. Disoriented himself, he tried to make sense of the incident, but soon the gas overcame him, and he stumbled back to Diffendorf Hall where collapsed on his office couch gasping for breath.

As soon as he regained his breath and his composure, he thought to try to locate Jefferson Drew and see if he needed any help. He expected Drew to be in the thick of the conflict, but because he was wearing a gas mask, he would be protected against the elements. Cotton rethought his prospect of aiding anyone and suddenly feeling nauseous, he decided to leave campus and go home. He was feeling guilty, climbing into his car, but decided he could do little to aid either side.

Instead, he cruised around campus looking to aid any student that needed it, but found most the demonstrators were holed up in buildings or behind makeshift barricades. Without much success, he decided to go home and lick his wounds. Now he had a job ahead of him, He would have to wait to see about certain developments, but he had to become the researcher again. Phone calls had to be made, people talked to and decisions to be made and some of them might lead Cotton to one of the most important decisions of his life.

Chapter 31

Aftermath

He drove back to his home in Wanakah in a semi-conscious state and was immediately put to bed by his concerned girlfriend. After he had related how he had been gassed and perhaps caught buckshot, she laid him down and stripped his outer garments to check for any wounds. After she was sure that he was not hit by any, buckshot, she covered him up and he drifted off to sleep.

He tossed and turned in a delirious state and finally fell into a deep sleep, punctuated by various faces and images. He saw police rising as gigantic figures carrying huge clubs smashing down on helpless victims. He pictured student demonstrators throwing more than just bricks and stones. They threw Molotov cocktails, incendiary devices of all kinds, including grenades. The two forces battled as the campus buildings came tumbling down. Both sides were consumed by the dust and rubble. It seemed to signify that in this instance, neither side would win, and the university would be destroyed.

Another image appeared beyond the rubble and dust. In the distance, two figures struggled. One of the figures eventually won out as the other tumbled to the ground. The remaining figure gathered up the body and slowly trudged away. Although both figures were indistinguishable, he could see that they both wore security uniforms At this point, the images dissolved, and Cotton fell into a more peaceful slumber.

The next day, Cotton was feeling much better and against Jen's protests, showered, had breakfast, and headed out to campus. It was a Saturday, so Jen did not accompany him.

On the ride in, his thoughts tumbled together in an avalanche of possibilities. One problem was the condition of the campus. In the aftermath of the demonstrations, what was going to happen to instruction and even more important, how could they keep both students and security safe?

He had two places he had to go. First Regan's office and then to see Drew.

Regan's secretary was off for the weekend. The door was open, and the lights were on in Regan's office. He heard Regan's voice and assumed he was with someone. However, the click of a telephone being placed in a receiver signified that Regan was now alone with his thoughts.

Cotton knocked on the door.

Regan saw who it was and sighed.

"For the first time in my tenure as president, I have no idea how to proceed. I was just on the wire to Albany with Rockefeller himself. He wanted to know the situation. I told him we were trying to pick up the pieces. He didn't like that. He said that if I couldn't handle the situation, I should consider alternatives."

Cotton sat down without being offered a seat.

"What is the situation out there, Cotton?"

"I think we're lucky it's Saturday. I think the students are licking their wounds. They realize that they can't win against a police force and the tactics they used yesterday. Buckshot and tear gas."

"The police deny they ever used buckshot," said Regan.

"I saw the wounds from buckshot on various students," said Cotton.

"I've already submitted my resignation effective at the end of the summer. I don't think I've failed. I think that I was dealt a stacked deck. I don't think anyone could hold this campus together. Student demonstrators, reacting to the whims of the war, Kent State and politics, city police and Erie County sheriffs, patrolling the campus. It was too much. I only hope we can make it to the end of the semester and clear out the campus."

"My hope too, sir. But there is another problem. These incidents against minority faculty members, they won't go away."

"I'm officially going against what I told you months ago. Do what you must. Use your contacts. Find the killer. Another death will cast a pallor over this campus that won't go away any time soon."

Cotton left the office determined to stop that from happening.

Chapter 32

Further Links

Cotton arrived at Drew's office in time to see him getting off the phone.

"Cotton, this whole thing is beyond me. Sitting here waiting for the next shoe to drop and now Barton."

"What do you mean, Barton?" asked Cotton.

"He's disappeared."

"I don't understand. It hasn't been twenty-four hours."

"We have a standing rule since early last fall. After a demonstration of any kind, we all report back to this office. He didn't show up. I called his house with no answer. I kept calling through the evening with no result. When he didn't show up this morning, I sent two of my men over to check things out. They knocked with no answer. Upon my authorization, they broke in and found nothing, His bed hadn't been slept in. We put an all-points bulletin out on his car with no result. He's disappeared."

Cotton took this news with no apparent surprise.

"What else can I do?" asked Drew with his hands up in the air.

Cotton offered no solution.

Cotton drove down the tree lined suburban street until he reached the address he was looking for. He had never been inside even though he knew the occupant very well. He decided to park a few streets away and walk in. There was no car in the driveway or garage as Cotton knew. He walked up the driveway past the front door and on to the back of the house. He hoped his entry into the back door would not elicit a neighbor's curiosity.

He came prepared with a few specialty keys that he had kept since his days with the Buffalo Police Department. He hoped they would work and that he wouldn't have to break glass. If he was wrong, he didn't want the person to think his house had been broken into.

Luckily the third key worked, and he entered a kitchen. Everything was neat and tidy. He continued through the house until he found what he was looking for-the entrance to the basement. He was careful going down the stairs, reaching the bottom and glancing around.

The basement stretched the length of the house with a few doors off to the side. He tried one and found that it held firewood and a chain saw. In the next one, he found what he hoped for. What he found was a crumbled body in a corner of a room no bigger than a closet.

He hurried over and checked on the pulse and found it weak but functioning. He rose with Barton's body in the beginning motion of a fireman's crawl when he heard a voice behind him.

"Damn it, Cotton. Now I have to kill you."

He turned around to see Jefferson Drew in the doorway with his service revolver pointed in Cotton's direction.

"Maybe I can work it out that you killed Barton and I killed you when you resisted arrest. Don't worry about it. An officer of the law is usually the last person suspected. And now, I have to say goodbye."

"Why you? What grudge could you have against all of those people, including Greg?"

"All of those people? All of those people? They didn't deserve it. None of them, especially back in Cleveland. But now, no more talking. I have an alibi to work out. And I really am sorry."

A shot rang out but not from Drew's gun. He tumbled to the floor and exposed a thin Black man in the distance. He moved into the doorway.

"Tried to wing him but I couldn't get the right angle. I finally had to settle for center mass, which was unfortunate for Drew."

"I know you," said Cotton. "You're Winston Scales."

"Right initials, wrong name. I'm Waylon Sands. Listen, hold the fort here, while I call an ambulance on the phone upstairs."

Chapter 33

Tying Up Ends

They were in Regan's office the next day – Cotton, Sands and the president.

"I was sent down here by Governor Rockefeller to find out what I could about the minority assaults. He couldn't let that happen on a State University campus. Of course, President Regan knew about my cover. I performed a few assistant duties just to justify my cover, but essentially, I was here to investigate. I was taken by surprise when I was assaulted in Allentown. I was lucky that some random pedestrians were passing by and intervened. I might have even caught him then, but he fled, and I was incapacitated. At that juncture, I knew things were serious. It was only during the last violent demonstration that I began to wonder. Who had access to various venues on campus like the chemistry labs? Who could move, without suspicion, across campus, to follow victims? He could always say that he was protecting them. Who was at that demonstration and could assault Lavelle Hughes? Who was at that final violent demonstration who could move about with impunity.? Who was above suspicion? That's when I, like Cotton, began to look into Drew's background."

Cotton picked up the narrative.

"A few calls to a Cleveland Police Department friend, Jim Davenport, completed the back story. Drew had been up for a promotion to Chief but was leapfrogged by Barton's father, Al, for the promotion. Drew was outraged and quit the department. He took the job at UB as head of security, but he later contacted Al Barton's son, who was estranged from the old man and told him that there was always a position to be had here on Drew's security force. The son, who was already on the Cleveland force, but chaffing at the bit under a father he didn't respect, took Drew's offer."

"What he didn't know was that Drew did this to be able to take revenge for what he considered a gross injustice in Cleveland. He wanted the young Barton close by. In the meantime, he found out that each of the minority victims on campus had got their position because they had jumped ahead of a more qualified white candidate. It was part of a new program by then President Meyerson called affirmative action. It enraged Drew to such an extent, that he decided to solve the problem by eliminating them all. I think, by this time, he had lost it."

"When things came to a boil with the latest demonstration, I thought it prudent to follow Drew. When I spotted Cotton's car a few streets over, I knew I had to go in," said Scales.

"Well, upon looking at Barton's record on the security force, I think he would be an able replacement for Drew. After he gets out of the hospital, I intend to offer him that position. And with a little luck, he just might be able to establish relations with some of the student radicals. I heard that he was doing just that before he was assaulted," said Regan.

Cotton left the building, tremendously relieved, the minority situation solved, students away for the summer, he just might be able to dedicate his time to his profession and Jen.

Chapter 34

August 20
Domesticity

It was the beginning of the semester, Cotton and Jen had been married at the end of June and the baby had come on the August 5, a smiling bundle of eight pounds ten ounces named Theodore Cunningham. His wife was taking her maternity leave during the fall semester and was being assisted by Teddy who was delighted by the new addition. Cotton's sister Connie had agreed that Teddy could live with them, although he spent as much time with Mrs. Davis next door as he did at the Cunningham residence. Both Mrs. Davis and Teddy were faithful companions to the new mother and baby.

Cotton and Jen were having a drink on the back patio one afternoon before classes started.

"Well Mrs. Cunningham, will you miss teaching in the fall?"

"I am going to enjoy this. With Mrs. Davis and Teddy catering to my every need and the weather being an extension of the summer, I might not want to go back," she joked. "I tell you one thing I won't miss."

"What's that?" asked Cotton.

She leaned over to take his hand.

"I won't miss the danger you've been in the past three years. I'll have you safe and sound by my side."

"Yes, you will," smiled Cotton. "Yes, you will."

Made in the USA
Columbia, SC
20 November 2024